"Whitney?" Drew looked at her closely.

"Did you hear me? I asked if you would consider marrying me to get custody of Elliot."

So, he *had* asked her to marry him. She slowly took a seat and stared out the picture window at the lush green grass and the perfectly sculpted hedge along one side of the property.

"No one has ever asked me to marry them before," she whispered. Not even Brock, whom she had dated for a year in DC. It had been two years since he broke it off, but she still struggled to trust anyone with her heart again.
It wasn't worth the pain.

Drew sat on the chair next to her, his shoulders rounded. "I know it's not the kind of proposal a girl dreams about—and you probably think I'm foolish to even ask you. I'm sure there are worthier men out there."

"It's not that." She turned to face him, not wanting him to think there was something wrong with him. On the contrary, Whitney had never imagined a guy like Drew Keelan asking her to marry him. She wasn't his type.

Gabrielle Meyer lives in central Minnesota on the banks of the Mississippi River with her husband and four young children. As an employee of the Minnesota Historical Society, she fell in love with the rich history of her state and enjoys writing fictional stories inspired by real people and events. Gabrielle can be found at www.gabriellemeyer.com, where she writes about her passion for history, Minnesota and her faith.

Books by Gabrielle Meyer

Love Inspired

A Mother's Secret
Unexpected Christmas Joy
A Home for Her Baby
Snowed in for Christmas
Fatherhood Lessons
The Soldier's Baby Promise
The Baby Proposal

Visit the Author Profile page
at LoveInspired.com for more titles.

The Baby Proposal

Gabrielle Meyer

LOVE INSPIRED
INSPIRATIONAL ROMANCE

LOVE INSPIRED®
INSPIRATIONAL ROMANCE

Recycling programs
for this product may
not exist in your area.

ISBN-13: 978-1-335-58689-6

The Baby Proposal

Copyright © 2022 by Gabrielle Meyer

For questions and comments about the quality of this book, please contact us
at CustomerService@Harlequin.com.

Love Inspired
22 Adelaide St. West, 41st Floor
Toronto, Ontario M5H 4E3, Canada
www.LoveInspired.com

Printed in U.S.A.

Pure religion and undefiled before God
and the Father is this, To visit the fatherless
and widows in their affliction.

—*James* 1:27

To Francess Janski.
Thank you for choosing me to be your godmother.
I love you.

Chapter One

Whitney Emmerson stood next to her rusted Volvo and stared at the elegant house in front of her. Behind the sprawling Cape Cod home, with its dormer windows, shingled siding and sloping eaves, was the sparkling Mississippi River. A vast lawn spread out on each side of the house and an equally charming detached garage sat to the right of the driveway. Whitney checked the address on the text one more time, just to make sure she was at the right place, and took a deep, fortifying breath.

The tears that had been threatening to

fall since she left Washington, DC, were still hovering at the backs of her eyes. She had forced them to stay in check for the past eighteen hours as she drove from her tiny apartment in Maryland to her sister's gorgeous house in Timber Falls, Minnesota. She had come as fast as the speed limit would allow, only stopping when absolutely necessary, but she had still not been here in time for the funerals.

A gentle breeze pushed against Whitney as she slowly walked toward the gray house. The sky was too blue and the sun was too bright on this early May morning. All around her, spring was blooming with hope and promise, yet inside, Whitney felt nothing but pain and darkness. Just twenty-two hours ago, she had received a phone call that had completely torn her world to pieces.

Her mom and dad, and her sister and brother-in-law had been in a car accident and none of them had survived. The only person who had, astonishingly, lived through the tragedy without a single scratch was Whitney's three-week old nephew, Elliot. A nephew whom Whitney had not yet met but had brought her rushing back to Timber Falls.

The front door opened and a man stepped out onto the porch.

Whitney paused at the sight of Andrew Keelan. He wore a pair of black trousers and a charcoal gray, long-sleeve golf polo. His dark brown hair was perfectly trimmed and his face was clean-shaven. She'd forgotten how handsome he was, though it had never been something she thought much about. They hadn't spent much time together, except for a few hours at her sister's wedding four years ago. Before that, he'd hardly known she existed. Whitney had been the maid of honor and Drew had been the best man, since his brother was the groom.

He was also the person who had reached out to let her know that her parents and sister were gone.

"Hi, Whitney," Drew said as he walked down the porch steps and met her on the cobblestoned driveway.

Whitney tried not to be self-conscious, but she had been on the road for over eighteen hours and hadn't slept in thirty-six hours. She'd been working a double shift at the Hard Rock Cafe when she got his call and hadn't had time to shower or change out of her work clothes before jumping into her car. She felt grimy and exhausted, a headache lingering behind her burning eyes.

"I'm sorry I couldn't get here in time." It was the first thing she'd said in hours and her voice was hoarse. Drew had tried to find her for days after the accident, but when he'd finally located her at work, it had been too late.

"It's okay." Drew's blue eyes were filled with compassion and grief. He had lines along the sides of his mouth and his eyes looked tired.

"If I had made an effort—" Whitney

pressed her lips together, not wanting to cry now, in front of Drew. She'd held it together this long. She could keep it inside for a bit longer, until she was alone. "If I had given my phone number or address to anyone other than Cricket, you could have found me in time." But she hadn't. The only person Whitney had spoken to since she'd left Timber Falls four years ago was her sister, and Cricket's phone had been destroyed in the accident. No one else knew how to get hold of Whitney, which was why he'd struggled to find her.

"You didn't know." Drew put his hands in his pockets and looked down at the ground, as if he was trying to collect his thoughts and emotions. "None of us knew something like this would happen."

Of course. Whitney had lost her parents and sister, but Drew had also lost his brother. His parents had both died years ago, before Cricket and Sam's wedding, which meant he understood Whitney's loss, too.

"I'm so sorry," Whitney said, wanting to reach out to Drew, but refrained. Though he was Cricket's brother-in-law, he was a practical stranger to Whitney.

"I'm sorry, too." He cleared his throat. "The funeral was yesterday. I'll take you to the cemetery, if you'd like, when you've had time to sleep."

She nodded. "I would like that."

"I imagine you're tired and would probably like to rest now—but there are a few things we need to discuss that can't wait. It's why I asked you to still come, even though I knew you couldn't be here in time for the funeral."

Whitney swallowed and nodded again. He had told her on the phone that he was the executor of Cricket and Sam's will and it involved her. He had asked how quickly she could get to Timber Falls and she had said she'd be there the next morning.

Now, here she stood, completely bereft and in a daze, wondering how to proceed.

"Let's head inside," Drew suggested. "We don't need to discuss this out here."

Whitney followed him toward her sister's beautiful house and she noticed her parents' large RV sitting along the back side of the detached garage. It prompted questions she wanted to ask, but there were so many other pressing matters to address, it would have to wait.

"Sam and Cricket bought this house last year, right before they found out they were expecting a baby." Drew opened the wide front door and stepped aside to let Whitney enter.

Though they didn't speak often, Whitney knew that Cricket had moved into the house. They spoke on the phone a few times a year, the most recent after Cricket had given birth to Elliot.

Whitney had no idea it would be the last time she'd hear her sister's voice.

The foyer was impressive with a grand staircase, a two-story ceiling and a glass chandelier overhead. Doorways opened up on either side, with one at the back of the room, but plastic was hanging from two of the doors and Whitney couldn't see what was behind them.

"They started remodeling about six months ago," Drew continued. "But the project kept getting held up for one reason or another. Cricket had hoped to be done before Elliot came along, but as you can see, it didn't happen."

Tools and sawhorses were stacked up on one side of the foyer while a painter's tarp covered the tile floor. There were a few different color swatches painted on one wall, as if they were still trying to decide on what color to choose.

"This is a beautiful house."

"It was the perfect spot for them, right along the river." Drew stopped and looked around the foyer. "It's near the sixteenth green and the cart path makes it—made it—easy access for Sam to get to the clubhouse to work."

Sam and Drew had inherited their family's golf course a few years before Sam and Cricket were married. Whitney had noticed that the house sat on the outer edge of the course as she'd pulled up to the driveway.

The couple had been perfect for each other. Both had loved the high-society lifestyle that came with their position in the community. A lifestyle that Cricket and Whitney had been raised in—but one that Whitney had never fit into. For the past four years, working in DC, Whitney had imagined her sister living a life just like this one. She would have been surprised to find out differently.

Drew led Whitney through a formal living room—which looked like it was almost finished, but had no furniture—and into a dining room that was finished and was furnished with a long, beautiful table.

Several folders and dozens of pieces of paper were spread out on the table. Drew pulled a chair away from the table and motioned for Whitney to sit down.

"Can I get you something to drink? Or eat?" he asked.

"What I'd like is a shower and a bed, but that can wait." Whitney sat on the front edge of the chair, her mind reeling. "I have so many questions."

"I'm sure you do." He took the seat across from her with all the paperwork laid out between them. A large picture window behind him showcased the manicured lawn and the river beyond.

She tried not to flinch or shy away from his gaze—but she hated that he was looking at her so closely. As if he was searching for something. And she was afraid of what he'd see: the parts of Whitney that no one had ever liked; the pieces of her that had never fit into the world her parents and sister inhabited—the one that Drew lived and breathed every day. But how could she hide it from him? No matter how much or how little he saw of her, he'd known, just like everyone else, that she didn't belong.

"I promise I'll answer all your questions," he said. "But I think the most important thing we need to talk about right now is Elliot—and who will raise him."

In all the pain and anguish, Whitney hadn't even considered what would happen to the baby. But now, it was all she could think about.

"Is he here?" Whitney sat across from Drew, her blond hair pulled back in a loose ponytail with tendrils of disheveled strands framing her face. She wore a pair of skinny jeans and a black T-shirt with a Hard Rock Cafe logo. The shirt had some stains and her mascara was smeared, but she looked as pretty as he had remembered from four years ago. He hadn't really known her before the wedding—or hadn't really paid much attention. His earliest memories of Whitney Emmerson were hazy and faint. He knew he'd seen her at the country club and around town growing up, but she'd been a kid.

When she walked into the country club to meet with her sister a few days before the wedding, Drew hadn't even recognized Whitney. She had just graduated college, if he remembered correctly. Her long blond hair had been down, reaching to the small of her back. Her brown eyes were framed in thick lashes and she had the brightest smile he'd ever seen. She wasn't what he'd consider a classical beauty, but more of a casual beauty with a girl-next-door kind of look.

From that moment on, Drew had been very aware of Whitney Emmerson.

But then, she had disappeared, right after the wedding. There had been a fight—at least, that was what he understood. Cricket never talked about it and Drew had never asked. And for the past four years, her parents wouldn't even bring up Whitney's name. But Cricket had. If her parents weren't around.

Now, here Whitney sat, across from him, looking lost and uncertain. He needed to tell her why he'd asked her to come all this way, as fast as possible. But it wouldn't be easy.

"Elliot has been staying with my cousin Paula," Drew began, "and her husband, Kyle, since the accident."

"Paula?" Whitney's face revealed her displeasure at the name. She wasn't fast enough to hide her response—and he wasn't surprised. Paula was a difficult person—had been since she was a child.

"How well do you know Paula?" he asked.

"We went to school together, but we weren't friends." Whitney lowered her gaze and wiped at a stain on her pants. "Our parents were friends and we vacationed together for most of our childhood, but she was Cricket's friend. They were on the cheerleading squad together, won the state golf championship in high school together, and were voted prom and homecoming queens their senior year in school. But Paula—Paula never liked me."

"If it's any consolation, she never really liked me, either."

The first hint of a smile tilted the corners of Whitney's full lips, though it didn't develop completely.

He studied her and she looked up to meet his gaze. She was several years younger than him—at least four, since she hadn't entered high school by the time he graduated. But at the age of thirty, it didn't really matter to him anymore. She was probably twenty-five or twenty-six, though she carried herself like a woman with a lot of life under her belt. There was wisdom and depth in the recesses of her brown eyes—disappointments and troubles he couldn't even begin to fathom.

She fidgeted under his gaze and he knew he needed to get to the point. She was exhausted and probably overwhelmed.

"None of us expected this," Drew began. "And I know it must be harder for you than anyone, since you lost your parents and your sister. Thankfully, Sam and Cricket had the forethought to create a will and they asked me to be the executor."

Whitney crossed her arms, as if shielding herself from whatever Drew was about to tell her.

"Sam and Cricket left all their property and assets to Elliot, and have asked me to be in charge of his estate until he reaches the age of twenty-five." He ran his hand over the back of his neck, trying not to feel overwhelmed himself. "There's a bunch of legal jargon here, but I just want you to know that no matter what, Elliot is going to be cared for."

"Good."

Drew watched her closely as he spoke again, his heart thumping a little harder at what he had to say next. "The will addresses who they would like to place as legal guardians over Elliot—which is why I thought you should come right away."

She swallowed hard and offered a slight nod.

"Sam and Cricket want Elliot to be

raised in a home with a married couple. They both desired a full-time mom *and* dad in his life." He knew that what he had to say might come as a surprise to her. "Their first choice to raise Elliot is you."

Whitney stared at Drew for a moment, unblinking, as if trying to comprehend what he had just said. "Me? Why would Cricket want me to raise her son?"

Drew frowned. "Why *wouldn't* she want you to raise him?"

"I'm the last person who would be up to their standards." She stood, her face filled with alarm. "I'm sure they want Elliot to lead the same lifestyle they led—and I—" She paused as tears formed in her eyes. "That's not me."

Drew also stood and walked around the table. He wanted to reach out and comfort her, but he hardly knew her. Countless people had come forward in the past week to offer Drew hugs, kind words and sympathy. Until today, he'd hardly been alone once. But had anyone hugged Whitney? Had anyone offered her sympathy yet?

"Cricket loved you very much, Whitney." He spoke softly, his voice earnest. "She talked about you all the time—had even tried getting your parents to reach out to you." The last part of his sentence sounded weak, even to his own ears. Cricket's parents had been living in their RV for the past year, coming and going since retiring. When Cricket learned she was pregnant, she had told her parents at a family dinner that it was time to set aside their differences with Whitney and reach out to her, but Mrs. Emmerson had put a stop to such talk. She had said they would wait until Whitney came to them— and only if she apologized first. Drew had wanted to ask what had happened between all of them, but he had kept his questions to himself. "Regardless, this is clearly what she wanted."

"It doesn't matter." Whitney wiped at her eyes and lifted a shoulder, a bit helpless. "Because I'm not married and I don't have any prospects."

Drew had been afraid she would say that. "The will stipulates that if you are not married, then their second choice is me."

"So, you'll make sure Elliot is cared for?" She looked at him hopefully.

He lifted his hands. "I'm not married, and I don't have any prospects, either."

"Oh." She put her hands on the back of the dining room chair. "Is there a third option?"

Disappointed, Drew nodded. "Paula is their third choice. And she *is* married."

"Oh," she said, a little more quietly.

"Yeah." Drew shook his head. "I'm going to be honest with you, Whitney. Paula and I have never been close. I don't like the thought of Elliot growing up with her as his mother." Not when Cricket had been such an amazing mom.

Until Elliot was born, Drew had never known what it felt like to love such a small and helpless little human. He hadn't spent much time around children before. His love for Elliot had been surprising—and now it was all-consuming. To know that the baby had no parents or grandparents was one of the most crushing realities he was dealing with right now. So much had been taken from Elliot, and Drew felt helpless. He would do anything to give the baby a happy family.

"What can we do?" Whitney asked. "It's what Cricket and Sam wanted."

Drew ran his hand over his hair and then rubbed the back of his neck as he contemplated their options—which were few.

The only serious girlfriend he'd had was in college when he was playing golf for the University of Minnesota. There had been talk that he could go professional, which had been his dream for as long as he could remember. His girlfriend had been supportive and cheered him on every step of the way. But then his dad had gotten sick and Sam had needed him to come home and help at their family golf course.

What should have been one summer turned to two after his dad died. And when Drew had decided not to return to competitive golf, his girlfriend had left him without a backward glance. It wasn't until that moment that Drew realized she'd been using him and piggybacking on his future success. He'd been leery of dating ever since, always wondering if someone had an ulterior motive for getting close to him.

"I've had almost a week to think about this," he said quietly, gently, hoping he wouldn't scare her off. "And I know you're hearing all of this for the first time, so you might need a little while to think it over. But—" He paused and swallowed, his heart pumping harder than it ever had. Not only for what he and Whitney would be risking, but what it all meant to Elliot, even though he didn't know it yet. "What if you and I got married—to each other?"

Whitney stared at Drew for a long time without speaking, and he was afraid he'd finally pushed her over the edge.

Chapter Two

Whitney was certain she hadn't heard
Drew correctly. Maybe the lack of sleep
was finally getting to her, or the shock of
learning she had lost her family. Whatever
it was, she felt like she was barely hanging on at the moment.

"Whitney?" Drew looked at her closely.
"Did you hear me? I asked if you would
consider marrying me to get custody of
Elliot."

So, he *had* asked her to marry him. She
slowly took a seat and stared out the picture window at the lush, green grass and
the perfectly sculpted hedge along one
side of the property.

"No one has ever asked me to marry them before," she whispered. Not even Brock, whom she had dated for a year in DC. They'd both been working at the Hard Rock Cafe, but he'd been a performer pursuing a record deal, and when he landed one, he had left her behind. She'd never felt so discarded—or heartbroken. It had been two years since he broke it off, but she still struggled to trust anyone with her heart again.

It wasn't worth the pain.

Drew sat on the chair next to her, his shoulder rounded. "I know it's not the kind of proposal a girl dreams about, and you probably think I'm foolish to even ask you. I'm sure there are worthier men out there."

"It's not that." She turned to face him, not wanting him to think there was something wrong with him. On the contrary, Whitney had never imagined a guy like Drew Keelan asking her to marry him. She wasn't his type.

"Proposing a loveless marriage isn't what I'd always envisioned, either," he said, sitting up a little straighter to look at her. "But I can't imagine Paula and Kyle raising Elliot—I just can't. It would destroy me, knowing I could have done something to prevent them from getting custody."

The passion and determination in his eyes were intense and it was clear how much he loved Elliot. Suddenly, all Whitney wanted to do was meet the baby and see him for herself. Did he look like Cricket or Sam? Would he have the Keelans' blue eyes or the Emmersons' brown ones? Was his hair dark or light?

"Can I meet him?" Whitney asked.

"Yes, of course." Drew nodded, as if he'd been remiss in not thinking of it himself. "I'll take you to see him right now—unless you'd like to rest first."

"No. I want to see him."

"They live on the other side of the golf course. It'll take just a few minutes to get there." He stood and Whitney followed—but then she paused.

"Can I clean up really quick?" The last thing she wanted to do was present herself to Paula looking like she did.

"Sure. You can use whatever room you want upstairs. None of them are being remodeled. Do you want me to get your bags?"

"There's no need." Whitney was used to doing things on her own, and she kind of liked it that way. "I'll only need about fifteen minutes or so."

"Take your time. I'll let Paula know we're coming."

Whitney went out to her Volvo and pulled her suitcase out of the back. She hadn't known how long she'd be in Timber Falls, so she'd only brought the necessities, but at least she had a clean pair of clothes to put on and her toiletries so she could brush her teeth and wash her face.

When she got back into the house, Drew wasn't in the foyer, so she walked up the grand staircase and down the hallway to look into the empty bedrooms. She found five of them. One was the master suite, which still looked like Cricket and Sam had left it. There were clothes hung over the back of a chair, a pair of shoes near the bed, and a jewelry box open on a bureau. Whitney's heart broke all over again, thinking about her sister, knowing they'd never talk or see each other again.

Whitney forced back the tears, trying to focus instead on Elliot and the question Drew had asked—the one she had skillfully avoided answering. Had he been serious? Would he truly consider marrying her, just to keep his nephew? What about love and romance? What if he met someone down the road that he truly wanted to marry? What would happen then?

There were no easy answers, so she pushed the questions aside and peeked into the next bedroom.

She paused, inhaling a breath, her heart melting a little at what she saw.

It was a nursery, decorated in khaki and muted blues. Whitney imagined Cricket's excitement as she planned and prepared her son's room. She was cast back to her childhood when she and Cricket used to play make-believe and they'd each have a baby doll in hand as they talked about what their lives would look like someday. Whitney had always thought that she and Cricket would be neighbors. They'd both be married and have lots of babies. During the day, they'd be in charge of the Parent-Teacher Association, and at night, they'd socialize at the country club like their own mom. But that had been before middle school, when everything had changed and the sisters were divided by social groups, their mother's expectations and life's disappointments.

Cricket had been living the dream they'd created in their make-believe worlds, while Whitney was living a far different reality.

She closed the baby's bedroom door and

entered the next bedroom, which looked like a guest room. There was an en suite bathroom, which she used to freshen up.

Fifteen minutes later, she met Drew on the front porch, feeling more human again.

He smiled when he saw her and she was struck, once again, by how handsome and clean-cut he looked. How was it possible that he hadn't been snatched up already? It seemed preposterous to believe that he had no romantic prospects—or that he'd want to saddle himself in a loveless marriage for the rest of his life.

"Paula said that Elliot is sleeping and she wanted us to come later," Drew said as he led Whitney to a golf cart she hadn't noticed in the driveway before. "But I told her we needed to see him as soon as possible."

"I appreciate that." Whitney hadn't been in a golf cart since she'd left Timber Falls. As she sat in this one, which was painted a dark, hunter green, she absently wondered how many miles she'd put on in golf carts like it during her childhood. Not only had her parents been avid golfers, and forced Whitney to take lessons, but she'd also worked as a beverage cart server during one of her summer breaks.

Drew maneuvered the cart down the driveway and onto the golf course, taking a well-maintained path between the holes.

"Do you know why my parents' RV is in Cricket's driveway?" Whitney asked.

"Your parents retired last year and sold their house. They've been living in the RV, driving all over the country. They were here when they found out Cricket was pregnant and then they returned this spring before Elliot was born."

"They sold our childhood home?" Whitney's mouth went dry, thinking about someone else living in the house she and Cricket had been raised in. They never talked about their parents when they called each other, so Cricket hadn't mentioned the sale of their house. What had her parents done with all of Whitney's childhood possessions? Had they thrown them out, like they'd thrown her out?

Drew didn't answer, probably because it was an obvious question. Instead, he waved at a group of golfers as they walked down the fairway toward the green, their golf bags over their shoulders.

"You and Sam have done a great job with the course," Whitney said, wanting to change the subject before she became emotional. "I've never seen it look this good."

"We're hosting a qualifying round for the PGA US Open three weeks from today."

Whitney's eyes opened wide as she turned to see if he was serious—and the look on his face told her he was.

"It was Sam's dream," Drew continued, his grief thick in his voice. "He was so excited. I can't imagine canceling it now. We'll hold it in his honor."

"That's amazing. I'm really impressed." Only the best courses were chosen for qualifying events.

Soon, they were pulling into a driveway on the other side of the course. The house wasn't as big as Cricket's, but it was still impressive and built into the hillside along the banks of the Mississippi River.

Drew parked the cart, and they got out and walked up the sidewalk to the front door. He pressed the doorbell and they stood back to wait.

Whitney wasn't sure what made her more nervous: seeing Paula again or meeting Elliot.

"You don't need to be nervous," Drew said, as if he could tell what she was thinking. "I'll be right here."

Warmth flooded Whitney at his words, making her feel less alone than she had in years. Though he hadn't asked her to answer his earlier question, she was certain it wasn't far from his thoughts. How could it not be?

The door opened and Paula appeared. She had aged a little since the last time Whitney saw her, but she still wore her auburn hair straight and perfectly parted on the side.

"Don't you know you shouldn't ring a doorbell when a baby is sleeping?" Paula asked Drew, as if he was completely inept. "I knew you were coming. It wasn't necessary to announce your arrival."

Drew inhaled and lifted his shoulders—but he didn't respond to her cutting words, instead he said, "Paula, you remember Whitney?"

"Of course I remember Whitney." Paula rolled her eyes impatiently, though she didn't even look in Whitney's direction. "What do you want, Drew?"

"We came to see Elliot."

"I told you he is sleeping."

"Isn't that what he does most of the day? We won't bother him. I just wanted Whitney to get a chance to meet her nephew."

Paula tapped her foot and crossed her

arms. Finally, she looked at Whitney, her lips pursed. "This is a little convenient to show up *after* your family dies. Were you too scared to face them after what happened?"

The words cut through Whitney's heart, but she wasn't ready to talk about what had happened—and most definitely not with Paula of all people.

"It's none of our business," Drew said to his cousin. "Let us see Elliot, please."

Paula rolled her eyes again and then turned and walked into her house, leaving the door open.

"I'm sorry about Paula," Drew said quietly. "She and Cricket were best friends and this has been especially difficult for her. She's been taking care of Elliot since the night of the accident."

"Does she know about the will?"

He nodded. "I told her and Kyle right away. They haven't been able to have any kids yet, and Paula is anxious to keep Elliot. When I told her I asked you to come, she threw a fit like I've never seen before. I'm sure that's why she's treating you the way she is right now."

Of course Paula would be upset—and to be honest, Whitney didn't blame her. Whitney wasn't fit to be a mother—but Drew *was* fit to be a father, and a much better option for Elliot than Paula.

They entered the house, but found Paula was already on her way up the stairs.

When Whitney and Drew got to the top of the stairs, Paula opened a door into a bedroom that had been darkened by shades at the window. It was a makeshift nursery with a pack-and-play crib, a glider rocker and a dresser with a changing pad on the top.

Paula stood back as Drew motioned for Whitney to follow him to the pack-and-play.

Slowly, Whitney peeked over the edge and her breath caught at the sight of her nephew.

He was sleeping on his back with his little hands balled up in fists near his chubby cheeks. He was so tiny, and so precious that Whitney's heart felt like it was going to explode with unexpected love. Though he was small, she could see that he favored Sam and Drew's family's coloring, with their dark hair and olive skin tone. More than anything, Whitney wanted to hold him, draw him close to her heart and feel a connection to her sister again. But she knew better than to wake him—and she was a little scared. She hadn't held a baby in years.

Drew lifted his hand to his face and when Whitney glanced up, she saw tears in his eyes. That was all it took to make the dam burst in Whitney's heart. The tears she'd been holding back for the past twenty-four hours could no longer be contained and they poured forth in quiet desperation down her cheeks.

Without a word, Drew pulled Whitney into his arms and held her tight. She wrapped her arms around his waist and pressed her cheek into his chest, thanking God for his strength and presence, knowing in that moment that her life had changed forever.

Drew had never cried in front of anyone before, not once during the long and nightmarish week he'd just lived through. To do so now, with Whitney in his arms, felt as natural as anything he'd ever done in his life. She, more than anyone, shared this heavy grief he'd been carrying all alone. For the first time since that horrible night when he'd been visited by the county chaplain at his apartment above the clubhouse, he didn't feel like he was doing this by himself anymore. Yes, there were others who had lost Sam and Cricket, but no one who was so closely connected to them and Elliot.

Thankfully, Paula had left the room, and Drew was able to hold Whitney for as long as they both needed.

Finally, she pulled back, wiping at her

cheeks. "Thank you," she whispered as she pressed her hand against his chest where her tears had wet the fabric of his shirt. "I'm sorry."

He put his hand over hers, feeling it against the beating of his heart, and shook his head. "You don't have to be sorry, Whitney. You can cry on my shoulder whenever you need to. We're in this together."

She looked up at him with her beautiful brown eyes, and he felt a bond with her that surprised him with its intensity.

"Can we go somewhere to talk?" she asked as she lowered her hand and glanced down at Elliot. "He looks so peaceful. I don't want to wake him."

Drew looked at his nephew again, thankful that the baby was so small he had no idea of the tragedy that had unfolded around him this week—yet heartbroken that he would never know his mom and dad. "Of course."

He led her out of the bedroom and found

Paula in the hallway, wiping her own tears. She pushed away from the wall and lifted her chin, almost in a look of defiance. "Well?"

"Well, what?" Drew asked, too heartsore to spar with Paula.

"Have you told Whitney who Cricket and Sam wanted for Elliot's guardians?"

"We talked about their wishes."

"And?" Paula impatiently wiped at her cheek again. "Is she married or not?"

"I'm standing right here, Paula," Whitney said, her voice filled with exhaustion and sadness. "And no, I'm not married."

Paula's shoulders fell in relief and she briefly closed her eyes. "So, what's our next step, then? Do we go before a judge to finalize custody?"

Drew's pulse picked up speed as he looked to Whitney, wondering if she was even considering his proposal.

She glanced up at him, and though she didn't communicate her feelings about it either way, he saw she was thinking about it. They studied each other for a heartbeat before Drew said, "Whitney and I have a few things to discuss first. How about we get together tomorrow morning with you and Kyle and let you know what we've decided."

Paula looked between Whitney and Drew, her eyes wide. "What do you mean you'll let me know what you've decided? What is there to decide? Neither one of you is married and Kyle and I are more than willing to keep Elliot. There's nothing to decide."

"Whitney has been driving for hours," Drew said. "She needs to get some sleep and then we can all sit down together to look at our options."

Whitney started to move to the stairway and Drew followed her. Paula stood for a second before chasing after them.

"What are your options?" she asked. "Neither one of you is married," she repeated. "The judge would never grant you custody with the stipulations in the will as they are."

"There is another option," Drew said as they came to stop at the bottom of the stairs. "I've asked Whitney to marry me."

If the baby hadn't been asleep upstairs, Drew was certain, Paula would have screamed. He saw it in the desperation in her eyes and the way her cheeks flamed with color.

"You've got to be kidding me." She said each word with calculated disdain. "You'd marry Whitney for the baby?"

Whitney lifted her chin and Drew took a step closer to her.

"If she agrees," he said, evenly, "I would be honored."

"What about Heather?" Paula put her hands on her hips and tilted her head, as if she'd found the loophole in his plans.

"Heather?" Whitney asked, looking toward him.

He shook his head. "Heather has nothing to do with this."

"She might not agree." Paula crossed her arms.

"Heather and I have no understanding or agreement," Drew said to Whitney. "She's the assistant clubhouse manager. We dated briefly, but it was several months ago." Heather Sinclair had been interested in Drew for a long time and Drew had finally agreed to go out with her a few times, but there had been no spark or sizzle between them. They were friends, but nothing more.

"If you're determined to get married to spite me," Paula said, "then why not marry someone you actually know?"

"I'm not trying to spite you, Paula." Drew sighed. "And this is between Whitney and me." He put his hand on the small of Whitney's back and walked her toward the door. "What time can we meet with you and Kyle tomorrow morning?"

Paula pursed her lips again, her arms still crossed. "Come by at nine—but Drew, consider what's best for Elliot and what Cricket and Sam really wanted. A *happily* married couple raising their son. Not a fake marriage of convenience to spite your cousin."

"Happily married" was a loose term for Kyle and Paula—at least, from what Drew had witnessed the past few years.

"We'll see you tomorrow morning. Thanks for taking such great care of Elliot." Drew opened the door and Whitney walked out in front of him.

Paula grabbed his arm and kept him inside for a moment longer, whispering, "You don't know what caused her to leave Timber Falls. You know nothing about her. Why would you risk your entire life's happiness on Whitney Emmerson?"

"Why would I risk not marrying her?" Drew had thought long and hard this week about proposing to Whitney if she wasn't married when he found her. He knew the pros and cons, the risks—and the rewards. He also knew that none of them had asked or expected this to happen, and as much as he was hurting, the real victim was Elliot. He would do anything for his nephew. Marrying Whitney to ensure that Cricket and Sam's wishes were met was the least he could do.

It helped that Cricket had spoken so highly about Whitney the past couple of years, making Drew wish he knew her better. Seeing her again today, though under difficult circumstances, made him even more sure of his choice. There was a gentleness about Whitney, and a quiet courage he admired. The bond he was feeling toward her was growing quickly, which encouraged him.

"I'll see you in the morning." Drew closed the door behind him and joined Whitney, who was already in the golf cart, staring at the river behind the house.

Whitney was quiet as Drew pulled out of the driveway and headed toward Cricket and Sam's house.

"She was right." Whitney crossed her arms, as if shielding herself again.

"Nothing Paula said was right."

"What do you think Cricket and Sam really wanted?"

"They wanted their son raised by you or me—Paula if nothing else." He wanted to convince her, but didn't want to push too fast, too soon. "If they knew we were going to raise Elliot together, I think they would be extremely happy. It's what they would want."

"You truly think that getting married is the best option?"

He felt her gaze on him, so he nodded. "I do."

"What if you find someone else down the road?"

He swallowed, trying not to worry about something that probably wouldn't happen. "I won't."

"You don't know that."

"How many people get married thinking they'll fall in love with someone else? No one."

"Most people who get married are deeply

in love with each other and aren't looking for a romantic relationship with someone else. We wouldn't be in a romantic relationship."

"No, but I would consider it a committed relationship."

"I wouldn't expect you to."

He looked at her quickly. "Are you considering my proposal?"

She nibbled her bottom lip for a moment. "To be honest, I don't have much to go back to in DC. I went there because a college friend had an apartment and needed a roommate, but she moved to Florida last year. I want to do something that matters with my life, and Elliot matters more to me than anything." She met his gaze. "But if we do this, Drew, we need to promise each other that we'll always be honest and open, no matter how uncomfortable or how awkward it might be. And——" She paused as she took another deep breath. "If you ever meet someone else that you'd rather be with, I will not stop you. I will get our marriage annulled and you can go on with your life—raising Elliot like I know he needs to be raised."

"I would never want to raise him without you."

"You deserve to raise him—more than I do. I would never agree to this if I didn't think you were the best choice. I'm only saying yes because he needs you."

"He needs both of us, Whitney."

"Do you agree to my stipulations?"

"That you'll get an annulment if I want one?" he asked.

"Yes."

"I won't want one—unless you also want the same stipulations for yourself? An annulment if you find someone else?" For some reason, that thought made him feel a strange twinge of discomfort, even though he hardly knew her. He'd been honest when he said that he would consider this a committed relationship.

She was quiet for a few seconds and then nodded. "Okay."

Drew pressed the brake on the cart and turned to give Whitney his full attention. "You'll marry me?"

Whitney suddenly looked shy as she uncrossed her arms. "I will."

"Good." A surge of excitement and energy rushed through Drew, surprising him with its intensity. This wasn't the kind of marriage he had expected, but the prospect of marrying Whitney and raising Elliot filled him with the greatest sense of purpose he'd ever felt. He'd made other sacrifices in his life, like giving up his chance at playing professional golf to run the family business, and though he'd been disappointed, it had ended up being the right choice. He suspected that this was going to be the same. There might be some sacrifices he was making, and a part of him was disappointed he wasn't entering a conventional marriage, but he knew it was the right choice.

"Good," she said, too.

He had the urge to kiss her, or to at least shake her hand to seal the deal, but nothing seemed appropriate, so he turned back to the steering wheel and held it for a second before continuing toward the house.

He was getting married. To Whitney.

A stranger, in almost every sense of the word.

Yet, one of the most intriguing women he'd ever met.

Chapter Three

Whitney opened her eyes the next morning as the alarm on her phone rang. She blinked a couple of times, trying to focus on the blue-and-white bedroom around her.

All at once, the memories from the past two days came back to hit her with a sudden pounding in her chest.

Her parents and Cricket were gone. And she was getting married today.

A burst of adrenaline raced through her from head to toe and she got out of bed with an energy she'd never felt before. Not only was she getting married at the courthouse at eleven, but by the end of the afternoon, she and Drew would pick up Elliot and bring him home.

She would be married and have a son when she went to bed tonight. It seemed like a dream. One part nightmare, one part fairy tale.

Whitney didn't have anything nice to wear to her wedding, so after her shower, she slowly walked into Cricket and Sam's bedroom.

The house was quiet, since Drew had gone home to his apartment the after-noon before to let her get some much-needed sleep. They had spent several hours looking over the will and the other papers Cricket and Sam had left behind. Drew had made a few calls to the court-house to see if they could get a license and schedule a ceremony with the justice of the peace. He had also called his best friend, Max Evans, who would come to the courthouse and act as one of the wit-nesses. Max's wife, Piper, would be the other witness. Whitney knew of Max—who didn't in Timber Falls? He had played professional football for several years before retiring. Drew had told her the rest of the story yesterday. After Max left the NFL, he had come back to Timber Falls to buy the bed-and-breakfast from his high school sweetheart, Piper, and they had eventually gotten married. Whitney didn't know them personally, because they were several years older than her, but she was happy they'd agreed to be witnesses.

There was no time to buy something decent for the wedding, and Whitney didn't really have the money to go shopping. She'd barely had enough cash to pay for gas on her way to Timber Falls.

That left only one option: to borrow something from Cricket's closet.

Whitney turned on the bedroom light and took a deep breath. She'd cried for hours last night after Drew had left, and wasn't sure she had any tears left inside her. Standing in Cricket's bedroom made her wonder if that was true. The emotions welled up again and she had to fight the grief as she walked across the room and into the gigantic closet.

A smile tilted Whitney's lips as she saw the organization and attention to detail inside Cricket's closet. It was full of designer clothing and expensive shoes and purses. Part of Whitney didn't want to invade this space, but the other part knew that Cricket wouldn't mind. She'd always been trying to get Whitney to borrow things from her in middle school and high school, complaining that Whitney's clothing made her look frumpy and unattractive. What Cricket didn't know was that Whitney loved her sister's clothes. She wore the frumpy garments just to be different than Cricket. She hated to be compared to her older sister, because she always fell short. First with her parents, then with her teachers, and then with the rest of the student body.

Now, standing among Cricket's things,

Whitney was reminded that her sister had been quite a fashionista.

Slowly, Whitney went through her sister's things until she found a dress that she loved. It was slate gray, with a design woven into the fabric. It had three-quarter sleeves and hugged tight at the waist, but belled a little until it reached her knees. The dress was semi-casual, but looked comfortable and still had the price tag attached. Somehow, choosing something that Cricket had never worn settled better with her conscience.

An hour later, she was dressed and waiting in the foyer, watching for Drew's car out the window. She had curled her hair and pulled half of it up. She had borrowed a pair of Cricket's black heels, which fit perfectly, and one of her handbags. She'd put on some makeup and felt a lot better today than yesterday, though it felt strange to be dressed up on a Wednesday afternoon.

A sleek, black car pulled into the driveway and Drew stepped out. He was wearing a dark gray suit, which looked like it had been tailored just for him.

Whitney caught her breath at the sight. He was so handsome it almost hurt to look at him and know this was not a love match but a marriage of convenience. Her heart pounded hard as he walked up the steps and she opened the door to greet him.

Drew paused on the top step, the surprise and delight in his gaze making her cheeks warm and her pulse race.

"Whitney." The one word was filled with awe. "You look stunning."

"Thank you."

She had always loved that moment during a wedding when the groom saw the bride for the first time in her wedding dress. And though this wasn't a traditional wedding day, and Drew wasn't in love with her, she knew she would never forget the look in his eyes when he saw her in this moment.

"Are you ready to go?" He motioned to

the car. "Max and Piper will meet us at the courthouse."

"I am." She closed the door and preceded him down the steps and to the car.

"I stopped by this morning and talked to Paula and Kyle," he said. "I just came from there." His voice was full of frustration and tension. "Paula was livid, but Kyle seemed to be relieved. I told them we'd be by to pick Elliot up after lunch, if that's okay."

Whitney nodded, swallowing the apprehension she felt in her gut. Were they doing the right thing? She had no idea how to care for an infant. What if something went wrong? What if they couldn't do this? Would Paula want him back? Was that even an option?

After Whitney got into the passenger seat, Drew closed the door and came around to the driver's seat. He got in and turned on the engine and then they pulled out of the driveway.

Fear and uncertainty twisted inside Whitney until she felt like she might be sick.

Ever so gently, Drew reached out and took one of Whitney's hands into his own.

She looked up at him, all of her concerns vanishing with the surprise of his touch.

"You're not alone," he said, looking into her eyes with compassion and understanding. "I'm afraid, too. But I know God has called us to this moment and He won't abandon us now."

His touch was tender and soft, and his hand felt strong. She turned her hand until their palms touched and entwined her fingers through his.

Warmth washed over her, comforting her and giving her courage she didn't know she possessed.

"Thank you."

"We're in this together, Whitney. I promise."

She wanted to throw her arms around him like yesterday, but it was impossible in the car—and probably wasn't a good idea, anyway. Her heart was softening toward Drew, but she knew it wasn't romance budding. It was more like comradery and a shared sense of purpose. Romance wasn't something she wanted or needed. It would only complicate their lives. Besides, she couldn't risk her heart. It had broken into a thousand pieces when Brock left her, and she still hadn't repaired it. She wasn't even sure if she could. Abandonment and rejection had turned her heart into something she didn't even recognize.

It didn't take long to reach the courthouse. Their first stop was the county recorder's office where they purchased their marriage license. They were assured there was no waiting time, so they went from there to their appointment with the judge in the courtroom where Max and Piper were waiting.

Max Evans was tall and muscular, with dark hair and a nicely trimmed beard and mustache. His wife, Piper, was tiny in comparison, but was as attractive as her famous husband. They were both dressed well and made an impressive image.

"Thank you for coming on such short notice," Drew said as he shook hands with Max and hugged Piper. "I know it was unexpected."

"This whole week has been unexpected," Piper said as she squeezed Drew's arm in empathy. "We're here for you, no matter what you need. And we don't have any guests at the bed-and-breakfast right now, so this worked out perfectly."

"I don't know if you remember Whitney," Drew said.

"Hi." Max extended his hand to Whitney. "I don't think we've met."

Whitney shook his hand. "I don't think we have."

"I remember you," Piper said with a smile. She offered Whitney a hug, which Whitney accepted. "I'm so sorry for your loss and the suddenness of all of this."

"Thank you."

Piper pulled back, but kept her hands on Whitney's arms. "If there's anything—anything at all—that we can do to help, don't hesitate to call on me. I was widowed two years ago and I understand the uncertainty death brings into our lives. I'm here to help."

Tears stung the backs of Whitney's eyes as she felt Piper's empathy and care. She nodded, unable to find the right words to thank her.

"Are you two ready?" Max asked, looking between Whitney and Drew.

Whitney glanced at Drew to see if he'd somehow changed his mind in the past few minutes, but he seemed as determined as ever to go through with it.

"I'm ready—if you are," he said to Whitney.

"I am."

Drew opened the door into the courtroom and held it for Whitney before Max took it from him.

The room was quiet and empty. At the front was the judge's bench and to the side was the witness stand and the jury box. There were a few other desks and then all the chairs for the audience. It wasn't quite what she'd hoped and dreamed for her wedding day, but nothing was playing out as she'd always expected. Besides, this wasn't a wedding in the real sense of the word—this was more like a business transaction. And what better place to do that than in a courthouse?

A door at the back of the room opened and the judge walked out—at least, Whitney assumed he was the judge, though he was wearing a simple suit and not his robes. He was a tall man, with a distinguished brow and dark eyebrows. He would have looked stern if he didn't smile at them.

"Mr. Keelan?" the judge asked.

"Yes, sir."

There were a few formalities the judge went through once his assistant arrived, and Whitney tried to focus on everything they said. Soon, the judge was asking her and Drew a series of questions, which they answered, and then they said some simple marriage vows. Within minutes, the judge was pronouncing them husband and wife and they watched as Max and Piper signed the marriage certificate as witnesses.

Everything was done efficiently and without any fuss. It was over almost as soon as it began.

When the judge said, "You may kiss the bride," Drew turned to look at Whitney, a question in his eyes. She found herself nodding, and when he gave her a gentle kiss on the cheek, her disappointment surprised her. Had she really thought he'd give her a kiss on the lips?

She hadn't expected any kiss at all—but what had she thought? A handshake? A curt nod? What did people do when they signed a legally binding contract?

"Congratulations," the judge said as

he shook their hands. "I will see that the custody papers are filed and will let you know when everything is finalized."

"Thank you." Drew nodded. "Please let us know if there's anything else we need to do."

The judge looked from Drew to Whitney, his face growing serious, his dark brows tilting into a frown. "If you decide to divorce or annul this marriage, and have no intentions of marrying anyone else, the child will be placed with Kyle and Paula Sumner. We will make sure that the late Mr. and Mrs. Keelan's wishes are to be honored, no matter the cost. Do you understand?"

Whitney's heart pounded hard at the severity of his tone, especially so soon after his congenial announcement that they were now husband and wife.

"Yes, sir," Whitney said, choking on the words as Drew nodded his agreement.

A few minutes later, they walked out of the courtroom, a married couple.

Even though Whitney didn't feel any different, everything had changed.

Drew didn't say anything as he pulled into the country club parking lot after their brief ceremony. Whitney sat quietly beside him, looking out the window, rubbing her left ring finger where there was no ring.

Guilt washed over Drew in a sudden wave of regret. He knew that their marriage had been the right thing to do—so then, why did he suddenly feel like he had cheated Whitney out of something really important?

Everything had happened so quickly. He hadn't really given the actual *wedding* much thought. There had been no flowers, no maid of honor, no congregation filled with the smiling faces of loved ones. Whitney hadn't been able to pick out a wedding dress, or choose her color theme. There had been no music, no wedding rings and no blessing.

She hadn't even really known the witnesses.

They were married in the eyes of the law, and that was about it. They had done the bare minimum to ensure custody of Elliot. But he didn't *feel* married. He hadn't really thought much about what it would be like to be married, because, until yesterday, he'd had no real prospects.

Now he had a wife—and a son.

"I hope you don't mind stopping at the country club for lunch." It was the first thing he'd said to her since they left the courthouse. "I told Max and Piper to meet us there. Treating them to a nice meal is the least I can do for their help today. And I figured we needed to eat. A lot of people have receptions at the clubhouse—not that this is a reception, I suppose. But, I thought we should mark the occasion somehow—"

"That's fine."

He had been rambling and appreciated that she had stopped him. "Then we'll go get Elliot. I'm planning to take the rest of the day off so I can move my things over to the house."

That statement brought her gaze around to his. "You're moving in?"

He opened his mouth to respond, but then stopped. Didn't she want him to live with her and Elliot? He had just assumed she would—but maybe she didn't.

"I thought it would be best, under the circumstances." He cleared his throat. "I want to be there to help with Elliot as much as possible. I'll still need to work at the golf course, especially as we get ready for the qualifying tournament, but I'll be home as much as I can be. I don't want you to feel the weight of all the responsibility."

She was quiet for a moment, so he went on.

"You don't mind if I move in, do you?"

"No. Of course not. It makes the most sense. And there's definitely plenty of room for all of us." She lifted her chin a little and took a deep breath. "I suppose we'll both have to get used to a lot of change. I've been living alone for the past year. It'll be strange to share a house with someone again."

"I've been living alone for eight years. It *will* be strange." But also kind of exciting. He liked the idea of seeing Whitney first thing in the morning and being with her and Elliot in the evenings when he came home from work. It would sure beat the lonely hours he spent by himself eating takeout from the clubhouse restaurant and watching the Golf Channel.

"I also called the contractor and they should be returning to the house today," he said. "They stopped working last week after the accident, but I want them to push full speed ahead and get everything done so they can get out of our way."

She nodded.

Drew parked the car and before he could walk around to her door, Whitney opened it herself and got out.

He was taken aback again by how pretty she looked today. The dress she wore fit her perfectly and her beautiful blond hair was curled and trailing down her back like it had that first time he'd noticed her four years ago. It was the most gorgeous hair he'd ever seen. Thick and silky, shimmering under the light every time she turned her head.

"You look really pretty today," he found himself saying without even realizing the words were going to come out of his mouth. He swallowed at the sudden attraction he felt for her—not that he hadn't felt it before, but it just seemed *different*, now that she was his wife.

Whitney met his gaze, something akin to embarrassment or pleasure warming her eyes. "Thank you. You look really nice, too."

He stood up a little straighter, hoping she wasn't just being polite. He liked the idea that his appearance pleased her, though he didn't know why it mattered so much. Whitney might be his wife, but she was not his sweetheart and he wasn't sure he'd ever have a sweetheart again.

Instead, he would look at Whitney as his friend—one he was growing more and more fond of with each passing moment. And one that he found very pretty.

She was holding herself with such decorum and grace it was a marvel to him, given the hardships she had endured this week. Yet, there was a wall around her. One she was clinging to with all her might. What would happen if he tried taking down that wall? Would she allow him to get close enough to know the real Whitney Emmerson?

Drew opened the clubhouse door, watching for Whitney's reaction to the remodeled space.

He and Sam had poured a lot of money into the clubhouse over the past couple of years, but it had been paying off. They had not only earned a spot as a PGA qualifying golf course, but they had people trav-

eling from the five-state area to play golf.
Business was booming and they were on
track to have their best year yet.

"Wow," Whitney said, opening her eyes
wide. "I love what you've done to the
place."

Pride lifted Drew's chest and he grinned.
"Really?"

"It's so elegant."

"We had a local designer work on the
plans. Her name is Liv Harris. She worked
with Cricket on the house, too, so she'll
probably touch base with you at some
point this week to go over the decisions
that still need to be made. I'm sure you
want to put your own style into the house."

Whitney lifted a shoulder. "It's Cricket's house."

He took her hand in his to stop her.

She looked up at him, surprise in her
gaze.

"From now on, it's *our* house, Whitney.
Yours, mine and Elliot's. I know it's not
what we all wanted, but it's what we have.

I want all of us to feel like we belong. Make the final decisions based on your own preference."

Tears welled up in Whitney's eyes, but she blinked them away and nodded. "Okay."

He smiled—really smiled. "We're going to be okay, aren't we?"

"I hope so."

Max and Piper had left the courthouse before Drew and Whitney, so they were already in the restaurant waiting. Drew had instructed the restaurant manager to reserve the best table, near the windows overlooking the Mississippi River. It wasn't the fancy reception Whitney deserved, but it was what he could offer her, under the circumstances.

Before they could get to their table, Drew and Whitney were stopped by Heather.

She walked around the corner of the pro shop, a clipboard in hand, and came up short.

Drew hadn't said a word to anyone at the golf course about his marriage. He hadn't even told the restaurant manager why he needed to reserve a table—so it was about to get real.

"Hey," Heather said to Drew, her curious gaze slipping over to Whitney. Heather was tall, thin and dark-complected. Her hair was almost black and her eyes were a deep, dark brown. She loved the game of golf almost as much as Drew did and she had been an assistant manager at the golf course for the past two years. They knew each other pretty well.

This would be a shock for her.

"Heather," Drew said, trying not to sound alarmed or uncomfortable at the realization that he would need to tell her about his unexpected marriage with Whitney at his side. "I'd like you to meet Whitney Emmerson."

Whitney stood quietly, clutching her black handbag, suddenly looking just as curious as Heather.

"Hello," Heather said, reaching out to shake Whitney's hand.

"Hi." Whitney accepted her handshake.

Both women looked at Drew to finish the introduction.

"Uh, Whitney is Cricket's sister," he said.

"Oh, I'm so sorry." Compassion filled Heather's face. "Everyone at the course is devastated. I can't imagine your loss. Nothing will be the same without Sam and Cricket."

Whitney nodded. "Thank you."

Drew cleared his throat, knowing he needed to be the one to tell Heather about the marriage. She'd learn about it soon enough and would probably have a lot of questions. Not only because he was her boss, but because they hadn't really clarified where they stood with each other. They hadn't been on a date in months, but they also hadn't really discussed things, either.

He decided to plow ahead. "Whitney and I were just married."

The look on Heather's face changed from compassion and empathy to shock. Her eyes widened and she paled. "What?"

"It was very sudden," Drew explained quickly. "We did it to gain custody of Elliot."

Heather's shock turned to confusion as she frowned. Drew could see there were dozens of questions on the tip of her tongue, but she kept them to herself. He'd have to talk to her about it, but right now wasn't the best time. Not with Whitney standing there and the Evanses waiting.

"Am I supposed to congratulate you?" Heather asked with an edge to her voice.

Whitney shook her head. "It's not necessary. Drew and I didn't get married for love, but for Elliot."

Heather nodded, though she looked completely adrift. Drew was sorry for her confusion and he didn't blame her. They should have talked, but they hadn't, and now there would probably be some hurt feelings on her part.

"We're going to eat lunch and then pick up Elliot," Drew said to Heather. "Please let the staff know I won't be in for the rest of the day. They should expect to see me at six tomorrow morning."

Nodding, Heather turned and left them, her back stiff as she walked away.

"I'm sorry," Whitney said to Drew.

"It's not your fault." He started to turn toward the restaurant, but she stopped him by putting her hand on his arm.

"If you want to back out at any time, I won't be angry or hurt."

He looked into her brown eyes and knew that she meant what she said, but he also knew something even more important. "We can't. If we do, we'll both lose Elliot. And we can't let that happen."

Whitney took a deep breath and nodded once.

Drew had married her for keeps—and

unless she wanted things to be different, then today was the first day of the rest of their lives.

unless she wanted things to be different, then today was the first day of the rest of their lives.

Chapter Four

Whitney stood next to Drew outside Paula's house for the second time in twenty-four hours.

"Are you ready?" he asked.

They had hardly finished their lunch when Drew had said it was time to get Elliot. He seemed anxious and Whitney completely understood. She had hardly touched her meal, knowing that they were expected at Paula's house to pick up the baby.

"I think so." She wasn't ready, but there was nothing she could do about it now. They were married and about to bring their nephew home.

Drew took a deep breath and then knocked on the front door. They waited for several minutes before Paula answered—and she seemed in no hurry to greet them.

"We're here for Elliot," Drew said to his cousin. "Is he ready to go?"

It was clear that Paula had been crying. Her face was red and puffy and she held a tissue wadded up in her fist. Whitney's heart broke for her. Even though she and Paula had never been friends, Whitney understood that Paula was grieving and she wasn't ready to give up Elliot. And despite the fact that she and Paula had never gotten along, the truth was that Paula and Cricket had been best friends. Paula had been there for Cricket over the past four years while Whitney was living in Washington, DC. Paula was probably heartbroken about losing Cricket—and equally devastated not to keep the baby.

Whitney completely understood the desperation to raise Elliot. Hadn't she just married a practical stranger to gain custody of the little boy?

Paula opened the door and then turned back into her living room. Elliot was already in his car seat, sleeping, his diaper bag waiting nearby. There was also a laundry basket full of bottles, formula, diapers, clothing, and other odds and ends that Paula must have taken from Cricket's house after the accident. "He's ready— though I doubt that you two are."

Drew went to the pile of baby items and picked up the diaper bag, putting it over his shoulder, and then grabbed the laundry basket. "Can you get Elliot?" he asked Whitney.

"Sure." Whitney walked slowly toward the sleeping baby, feeling Paula's eyes burning into her back. Slowly, Whitney picked up the car seat, trying not to disturb Elliot. He had a little pacifier in his mouth and when she accidentally bumped the car seat against her leg, the baby began to suck harder on the pacifier—but he didn't wake up.

"When was the last time he ate?" Drew asked Paula, stopping near the door.

Paula wiped at her nose with the tissue and lifted her chin. "About an hour ago."

"How soon will he need to eat again?" Whitney asked.

"He'll let you know." It was all Paula said—all she appeared to want to say. She kept her lips sealed as she watched Whitney walk toward the door.

There were so many other questions Whitney wanted to ask, but she didn't think Paula would cooperate, even if she tried. Like, how often did he need his diaper changed? When would he need a bath? How did she mix the formula for his bottle? How were they supposed to secure the car seat into the vehicle? How often did he sleep and what was the best way to get him to sleep? Where did she buy his diapers and formula?

Anxiety started to creep up Whitney's

legs as the questions piled higher and higher. There was no way they were going to be able to do this—unless Drew knew more about babies than she did.

"Thank you," Drew said to Paula. "We really do owe you a debt of gratitude."

"If you cared for that baby, even just a little," Paula said, shooting darts from her glaring gaze, "you wouldn't be taking him from me."

Whitney looked to Drew for his response. He shook his head. "I love this baby more than life itself," he said. "And I believe that Sam and Cricket would be happy with Whitney and me raising their son. He will be the most important thing in our life from this moment on."

Paula crossed her arms and walked out of the room.

Drew glanced at Whitney and she could see that he felt bad about Paula, too—yet, what could they do about her sadness? This was what Cricket and Sam wanted—

kind of. They were doing the best thing for Elliot, weren't they?

She hoped and prayed they were.

Whitney followed Drew out to the car and watched as he popped the trunk and put the diaper bag and laundry basket inside. When he finished that, he opened the back door for Whitney.

"Do you know how to fasten the car seat?" he asked her.

"I have no idea."

He had the cutest frown as he studied the car seat for a few seconds and then said, "For now, let's attach the seat belt through here." He pointed to a section that looked like a seat belt would fit. "And when we get back to the house, I'll watch a YouTube video to see how it's done properly."

"Do you think it'll be okay?"

He met her gaze. "I hope so. Thankfully we don't have far to go."

"I'll sit in the back with him to make sure he's okay."

Drew took the car seat as Whitney

climbed into the back seat, then he put Elliot into the vehicle and attached the seat belt like they had discussed. It looked secure, but Whitney couldn't be sure.

"I'll go slow," Drew said as he pulled out of the driveway a few seconds later.

When he said he'd go slow, he wasn't joking. Whitney had never been in such a slow-moving vehicle. The short ride back to the house, which took about five minutes at regular speed, lasted almost twenty.

Once they were in Sam and Cricket's driveway, and Drew parked the car, he came around the back and took Elliot and his car seat out. After handing the baby off to Whitney, he took the other items out of the trunk, and then the little makeshift family—for that was what they were, though it was still hard for Whitney to comprehend—walked into the house.

"I'll go set his things up in his bedroom," Drew said.

"Where should I put him?" Whitney

looked down at the infant who was still sound asleep. "Should I leave him in his car seat?"

Drew stood in the entryway, his hands full, and shrugged. "Maybe we should put him in his crib, since he's sleeping."

That seemed like a logical thing to do with a baby.

Whitney followed Drew up the stairs and into Elliot's bedroom. As he set down the baby items, Whitney put the car seat on the floor and then stared at the contraption keeping him locked into place.

Drew stood beside her, staring at it, too.

"Have you operated one of these things before?" she whispered to him.

"I saw Cricket and Sam put him in and out of it. I think I know how it works."

Whitney took a step back and motioned for him to proceed.

He bent down and pushed a button in the middle of the harness and then pulled it apart. After that, he pushed the other button near Elliot's chest and popped the two sides out.

Elliot stirred in his seat and made a little grunting noise. The sound of it went straight to Whitney's heart. She'd never heard something so adorable in her life.

Slowly, Drew removed the baby from the car seat.

He was so tiny and his little legs were scrunched up as he arched his back and yawned, causing his pacifier to slip out of his mouth. Thankfully, it was connected to a ribbon that was attached to his sleeper. His face bunched up and turned red, but before he could start crying, Drew put the pacifier back into his mouth and Elliot calmed again.

"Want to hold him?" Drew asked, looking up at Whitney.

She hadn't held a baby in years, and she remembered that the last one had cried and cried. Whitney had been certain she was the reason the infant had screamed and she hadn't offered to hold another one since then.

But this was different. This was her nephew—her responsibility. She'd have to hold him eventually.

Slowly, Whitney nodded, her hands trembling at the reality of this moment.

With more gentleness than Whitney could imagine, Drew placed Elliot in her arms.

The baby kept his legs pulled up to his belly as Whitney held him. She tried not to feel—or look—awkward, but it seemed an impossible feat.

Without opening his eyes, Elliot turned to nuzzle his face against Whitney's arm and opened his mouth so his pacifier fell out again. Within seconds, he started to cry.

Whitney went rigid as she looked up at Drew. "What did I do wrong?"

Drew simply shrugged.

The baby nuzzled against Whitney's

arm with more ferocity and determination, crying even harder.

"Here," she said as she handed him back to Drew.

He took Elliot, but the baby did the same thing to him.

"Does he want something?" Whitney asked over the sound of the cries.

"I have no idea." Drew began to bounce the baby gently and then lifted him slightly to sniff at his diaper. "He doesn't smell."

Despite the crying and uncertainty, Whitney found herself smiling at the comical relief she saw on Drew's face. "That's good." She got close to Drew and the baby and tried putting his pacifier back in his mouth. He latched on to it desperately, but after sucking on it a couple of times, he began to cry again. "Maybe he's hungry."

Drew nodded. "That has to be it."

Whitney went to the basket of items on the floor and took out a small bottle and a jar of formula. "How do we make the bottle?"

"Are there instructions on the packaging?"

Of course. Whitney shook her head. She was an intelligent woman who had been managing life on her own for years. She should be able to figure this out.

"One scoop of powder for every two ounces of warm water." She looked at the bottle, which held four ounces. "Should I just make two ounces, or should I make the whole four?"

Elliot's cries were growing more desperate by the minute.

"Might as well make four," Drew said, bending his knees to bounce Elliot deeper. "I'd rather have too much than not enough."

There was a gallon of distilled water in the laundry basket, which Whitney assumed was for the formula. But how to heat it? She looked back at the packaging and it said not to microwave but to heat the bottle in warm water.

After mixing up the right amount, Whitney hurried into the bathroom and ran the bottle under hot tap water. Every few seconds, she checked the warmth of the formula on her wrist, knowing at least that much from watching movies and television. When it felt warm, but not hot, she went back into the nursery where Drew was starting to look as desperate as Elliot sounded.

She handed the bottle to him and he placed it into Elliot's mouth.

The baby latched onto the bottle as if he'd never eaten before and sucked on it with gusto.

Soon, the sounds of his cries were replaced by the sound of him swallowing the milk.

After a few minutes, Drew looked up at Whitney, a wobbly smile on his face. "Our first crisis averted."

She met his smile, feeling extremely accomplished, though it was a small task. "I plan to study as much as I can tonight about caring for an infant. Maybe tomorrow I won't feel so inadequate."

But who was she kidding? No matter how much she studied, she'd never be prepared to be Elliot's mom.

The evening was cool as Drew stepped out onto the back patio. Overhead, the moon was so full and so bright it cast shadows onto the manicured lawn behind the house. A tail of light trailed in the river, moving with the current.

"I brought you some hot chocolate," Drew said as he handed a mug to Whitney. "I didn't know if you liked coffee or tea, but I figured, almost everyone likes hot chocolate."

Whitney looked up at him, surprise on her pretty face. "That's thoughtful. Thank you. I love hot chocolate."

"Mind if I join you?"

She was sitting next to the gas fire table, which she had lit, and had her cell phone open to a parenting article, if he wasn't mistaken. "Of course not."

He sat next to her on the outdoor couch. "Learning anything good?"

She turned off her phone and set it on the end table next to her. "There's so much to learn. I'm in over my head, and I think Elliot can sense it, too. He knows we're imposters."

"Then that makes two of us—in over our heads, I mean." He took a sip of his hot chocolate and sighed. On the end table was the baby monitor, which had a video of Elliot sound asleep in his crib. He looked so tiny and defenseless. "Aren't all first-time parents in the same boat as us?"

"Maybe, but they usually have nine months to learn everything they need to know. We've had twenty-four hours."

The air was still, for which Drew was thankful. It would have been too cold to be outside if the wind had come off the cold river. Even with his parka, it was chilly. He wasn't sure why Whitney had chosen to come outside, when she could be in the warm house.

"It's so peaceful out here," she said almost to herself, as if reading his thoughts. "I've always loved the Mississippi River. I missed it when I was in DC."

He'd been wondering about her life in DC. They hadn't had much time to visit during the afternoon as they had met Elliot's needs and he'd moved some of his things into the house. He had decided to take the other guest bedroom, even though it was farther away from the nursery, because the thought of sleeping in Sam and Cricket's bedroom was just too much, on top of everything else. It would probably be a long time before they were ready to move Sam and Cricket's things out of the house.

But now, after Whitney had cleaned up their simple supper of spaghetti and meatballs, and he'd fed and changed Elliot one more time, he felt like there was a little breathing room to get to know each other better. Though how much she was willing to share with him was yet to be determined.

"How did you like living in DC?" he asked.

She stared out at the river and sighed. "To be honest, I wasn't a big fan. I loved it at first, with all the things to do and see, but after a while, I felt trapped. I prefer small-town life to a big city."

Drew nodded. "Something we have in common." He took a sip of his hot chocolate, enjoying the flavor and heat it offered. "If you didn't like it, why'd you stay there for so long?"

She sipped from her mug and brought her focus back to him. "I got stuck in my ways there, I guess. I had a job and a place to live. I made a few friends." She shrugged. "It seemed easier than anything else."

"Weren't you a music major in college? I

think I remember hearing that you wanted to be a teacher or something. I even remember Cricket telling me you wanted to start your own music school one day."

She looked away again and shook her head. "I haven't touched a piano or sung a note since I left Timber Falls four years ago."

Drew frowned and leaned forward. "But weren't you teaching music in Minneapolis, right before the wedding? I thought you were trying to get financing for a school."

"A lot of things happened before the wedding," she said. "But a lot changed after. I had an internship at a music academy in Minneapolis that summer—but I didn't pursue teaching music in DC. I worked at the Hard Rock Cafe—it paid the bills."

He still had no idea what had driven Whitney away from her hometown, but he wasn't sure right now was the time to ask. They'd been through a lot in the past couple of days and they had the rest of their lives to ask each other tough questions.

"My dream was always to play professional golf," he offered, hoping that his vulnerability would make her feel comfortable to share with him. "I did some amateur competitions in college, but I stopped competing once I moved home to help with the golf course."

"You're really good—that much about you I know."

"And you're a really good singer," he countered. "Cricket talked about it all the time."

She studied him in the flickering light from the fire table, as if she was contemplating whether or not to travel down that road. Finally, she said, "Why didn't you pursue your golfing dreams?"

He hadn't shared this much about himself to anyone else. Yet, if he and Whitney were going to become a family—as strange as that sounded—then he needed to be open with her.

"The dream to be a golfer is alive in here." He pointed to his heart. "But as soon as I actually *try* to be a professional golfer, and I fail, then it dies. And that thought terrifies me. I'd rather live with an unfulfilled dream than a dead one."

Whitney's brown eyes were filled with compassion and understanding as she nodded, her lips coming up into a sad smile. "I know exactly how you feel. I might not have been willing to admit it to myself when I was in DC—but it's true."

He studied her for a moment, believing with all his heart that she *did* understand. And for the first time, he felt safe leaving this piece of his heart with someone else. He knew she was trustworthy, because she was struggling with the same issue.

"Is it ever too late?" she asked. "Too late to realize our dreams?"

Was it? He had a US Open qualifying event on his own golf course, yet he was terrified to sign up. It had been easy to come home from college and use his father's illness as a guise for putting off his dream, but how long could he use that excuse? He wasn't getting any younger— and an opportunity to try again was knocking on his front door.

"No," he finally said, knowing she needed to hear the truth as much as he did. "It's never too late to follow our dreams."

"And even if we don't succeed the first time," she said, as if she was trying to convince herself, "that doesn't mean the dream has to die, right? There's no time limit or attempt limit, is there?"

He shook his head, starting to believe what he was about to say. "No. I don't think there is. History is full of people who didn't achieve their dream until they were older."

"Good." She looked down into her hot chocolate. "Because I can't believe that my dream to teach music is dead. I just can't."

Neither could he.

Maybe God had brought Whitney Emmerson—Keelan—into his life to remind him that nothing was completely lost. And nothing was too late.

Chapter Five

A baby's cries startled Whitney out of a heavy sleep, and for a moment she couldn't remember where she was or why there was a baby crying.

Grabbing her phone, she looked at the time and saw it was five thirty in the morning. She also had a text message from Drew—pulling her out of her deep sleep and back into reality.

Good morning, Whitney. I hope this text doesn't wake you up. I'm heading to the golf course. I'll be home around three. Don't hesitate to call or text me if you need anything.

Whitney rubbed her eyes and then looked at the time stamp on the text.

Five fifteen.

Wow. That was an early start.

Elliot's monitor was right next to her phone and she could see him flailing his arms and legs in his crib as he cried.

He seemed to be calling for an early start, too.

It was still dark, but that didn't seem to bother anyone else, so Whitney got out of bed and plodded down the hall to the nursery.

"Shh," she said as she went to Elliot's crib. "I'm here. You're not alone."

The sound of her voice seemed to calm him—and then she remembered how everyone had always told her that she and Cricket sounded so much alike.

Did Elliot think she was his mom?

Grief hit her hard and unexpectedly, bringing tears to her eyes and a lump in her throat. Yet, there was no time to weep. At least, not now. Elliot needed her to be strong and capable—to love him like

Cricket loved him and to care for him as only a mother could.

She lifted him out of his crib and bounced him gently at her shoulder. His sleeper was wet and he nuzzled her neck, looking for something to eat.

"I can't feed you until we get you cleaned up," she said to him. But how was she supposed to give him a bath? They hadn't needed to yesterday.

The thought of doing it without Drew was more daunting than ever. Yesterday, they had been a team. Today, Elliot was her sole responsibility.

It took Whitney longer than it should have to find all the necessary bath items and get the baby undressed. She filled up the tub with one hand while cradling the baby with the other.

And when she finally got Elliot into the tub, with him crying the whole time, he decided to take that moment to urinate again—and this time, it got all over her.

"Oh no!" she cried out.

Elliot wailed even harder.

Tears of frustration sprang to Whitney's eyes for the second time that morning as she tried to speak in low, soothing tones to the frightened baby.

Nothing seemed to pacify him, so she quickly finished his bath, put a fresh diaper on him, wrestled him into a clean sleeper and then made a bottle.

Finally, as the sun crested the horizon, she was sitting in the rocking chair in the nursery, feeding Elliot and enjoying the relative silence once again.

The two of them must have dozed off in the chair, because she awoke much later to the sound of the doorbell. It startled Elliot, who began to cry.

Whitney set aside his empty bottle and found his pacifier. That seemed to appease him for the moment as she went down the stairs to the front entrance. Elliot fit snug in her arm and stared at her with his big brown eyes.

Without even considering her appearance, Whitney opened the front door and was met by a man in a pair of jeans and a T-shirt that said Horton Construction.

"Morning," he said as he looked her over from head to foot.

She finally realized what she must look like, having practically fallen out of bed at five thirty—not to mention that she hadn't taken the time to change since Elliot had urinated on her.

Whitney touched her hair, though it was a feeble attempt to pull herself together.

"I'm Rich, the contractor. Drew said we should come back today." He squinted as he met her gaze. "Weren't you expecting us?"

"Yes," she said. "Of course. Come on in."

Rich called to his team, who were waiting near a couple of vans and a pickup truck. "All clear. Time to get in and finish up this project for the Keelans."

The Keelans. That was her, Drew and Elliot. She had decided to take on their last name, to make things less complicated—but it still felt strange to think of herself as a Keelan.

"I'm going to go lay the baby down," she said to Rich. "And jump in the shower."

"Okay—but we need to have a meeting as soon as possible. There are a lot of decisions to make and we promised Drew we'd get this project buttoned up as soon as possible. I need to know your answers before my crew gets into the thick of things."

Whitney's arm was getting sore from holding Elliot, and she desperately needed to clean up before she could even pretend to think.

"Fifteen minutes is all I need," she said as she started back up to the stairs. "Can you give me fifteen minutes?"

"Sure. I'll have my guys start hauling in the tools. That should take a little time."

"Thanks."

Twenty minutes later, Whitney was back in the foyer, showered and dressed, though her hair was still wet and lay against her back. Thankfully, Elliot had fallen asleep when she'd put him in his baby swing. The contraption was impressive, with several settings, music, and even a built-in bouncer.

"Oh, there you are," Rich said when he caught sight of her. "The carpet layers are coming tomorrow, so we need to finish painting the living room and study. Cricket—" He paused as he looked down for a second, and then continued. "She hadn't decided between two colors."

Rich pulled two paint chips off his clipboard and handed them to Whitney. They were almost the same shade of gray, though one had a bit more brown and the other more of a green tint to it.

"Which one—or do you want something else entirely?" Rich asked. "I need to send one of my guys up to the paint store right away."

Whitney had no idea what color the carpet would be, or what color the furniture was—if there was furniture. Surely

Cricket had moved it out and it was in storage somewhere?

The doorbell rang.

"Can you hold on for just a second?" she asked him.

"I need to send my guy—"

"I know—just a second." Whitney went to the door and opened it. There was a large moving truck in the driveway with a furniture store logo on the side. Two men were standing on the front porch.

"We're here with the living room furniture," one of the men said to her.

"Living room furniture?"

The guy looked down at his clipboard. "Ordered by Cricket Keelan six weeks ago. Delivery scheduled for today between eight and noon."

Whitney put her hand to her forehead. How many other things would show up that Cricket had planned? No doubt the painting and carpet were supposed to be finished last week, in time for this delivery.

She tried to explain the situation to the deliverymen, and they seemed truly sympathetic, yet, one of them explained, "I understand your dilemma, ma'am, but unfortunately, we charge by the mile and this furniture came from forty miles away. If we have to restock it, there will be another fee, and if you decide to have it delivered again, that'll cost you."

The baby monitor started to vibrate, which meant that Elliot was fussing again.

Whitney wanted to sit down on the floor and start to cry.

"There should be room in the garage," Rich told the deliverymen. "If that's okay with you," he said to Whitney, "we can haul it into the house tomorrow after the carpet is laid."

She could have hugged him right then and there. "Yes. Thank you."

The men nodded and made their way to the van.

At that moment, another unfamiliar car pulled into the driveway.

What now? Rich was still waiting for an answer and Elliot needed her.

She couldn't deal with one more thing. She was about to close the door on the unwanted visitor when she realized who had come.

It was Piper Evans. And she had a smile on her face and a baking pan in one hand.

"I've come to help," she called out to Whitney when she met her gaze, while lifting the pan up for inspection. "And, I've brought supper."

For the second time that day, Whitney wanted to hug someone—and when Piper got inside the house, she did.

Every time Drew tried to leave his office, something else came up, demanding his attention.

He looked at the clock on the wall and saw that it was already fifteen minutes past three, and he'd promised Whitney he'd be home at three. No doubt she needed a respite from taking care of

Elliot, and truth be told, Drew missed them and had been ready to go home hours ago.

"Knock, knock," came a feminine voice at Drew's open door. "Can we talk?"

It was Heather.

Drew had been avoiding her most of the day, needing to catch up on a week's worth of work—both his and Sam's. He hadn't wanted to deal with the inevitable conversation he needed to have with his assistant manager. At least, not today.

"Now isn't the best time to talk," he said as he turned off his computer monitor. "I'm on my way out."

"Heading home to the wife?" She tried to chuckle, but it fell flat.

"Actually," he sighed as he stood, "I am. She expected me at three."

Heather walked into Drew's office, though she left the door open. "What I have to say can't wait. I'm giving you my resignation. I'll stay until after the PGA event, but then I'll be leaving."

Drew stopped putting his papers in order and stared at her. "You have to be kidding me. You're the best assistant manager we've ever had—and I desperately need you now that Sam's gone."

Heather looked down at the desk and toyed with a paperweight. "I really don't think I should stay under the circumstances."

"What circumstances?" Though he knew what she was talking about, he hadn't really thought that marrying Whitney would cause Heather to quit her job.

"Your marriage, Drew. What else? Didn't you think I'd care that you up and married a stranger—over someone like me?"

"Would you have married me if I asked?" It was a rhetorical question, since he would never have asked.

She lifted her hands. "Probably not—but that's beside the point."

"I needed to get married to keep Elliot—and Whitney is his aunt. Sam and Cricket wanted us to raise him."

"What about you and me?"

Drew shook his head and lifted his shoulders. "I don't know what you mean."

"I thought things were...progressing."

"We went out a couple times a few months ago. I figured that you knew how I felt when I didn't ask you out again."

"I thought you didn't ask me out because we see each other every day." She finally met his gaze. "I really like you, Drew."

His discomfort was growing by the moment. "You're the best at your job, Heather. No one would deny that. But I really don't think you and I would have been good together. And it doesn't matter much anymore, because I'm married."

"Which is why I'm leaving. I'll have a letter of resignation on your desk tomorrow."

"Please don't. I need you right now—the course needs you," he corrected himself. "I can't lose anyone else."

"You should have considered that before you married Miss District of Columbia."

"Hey," he said, surprising himself with the sense of protection he felt for Whitney. "She's my wife."

Heather gave him one long look and then turned on her heels and left his office.

Disappointment and stress mounted in Drew's chest. Heather really was the best assistant manager that had ever worked at the course. He hated the thought of losing her—but he was thankful she was willing to stay until the qualifying event was over. Maybe if she had some time to cool off, she'd consider staying on afterward.

But that was something Drew would have to worry about later. He needed to get home to Whitney and Elliot.

A few minutes later, he was on his golf cart, driving across the course toward home.

Home.

It was such a strange word to him. For

years, he'd been living alone in an apartment. Now he not only had a beautiful home to go to, but a wife and a baby, as well. How long would it take before that didn't sound odd to him?

Horton Construction vehicles were in the driveway as Drew pulled the golf cart to a stop near the garage. He pressed the garage door opener and was about to pull the cart inside when he noticed all the furniture sitting there.

Lifting an eyebrow, he closed the door again and left the cart outside the garage.

The sun was high in the sky and it was getting warmer as he walked up the front porch and into the house.

Construction workers were everywhere. In the foyer, in the living room and in the study. Some of them nodded recognition at Drew, but most of them didn't seem to notice his arrival. Rich was the only one who approached.

"How's it going?" Drew asked the contractor.

"Well," Rich said as he stuck a pencil into his back pocket. "We had a rough morning, but things turned around after a bit."

"Rough morning?"

"Whitney was a little overwhelmed with all the decisions, but she rallied."

"Do you know where she is?"

"Last I saw, she was in the laundry room."

"Thanks." Drew had been worried about her all day, knowing how overwhelming it had been for both of them to care for Elliot together. He couldn't imagine how much more difficult it would be on her own. If he could have avoided going to work for one more day, he would have—but with the PGA event right around the corner, and the work that had accumulated since Sam's death, there was no way to put it off.

He walked toward the kitchen and the laundry room just beyond.

Natural lighting filled the bright room

where he found Whitney humming to herself as she folded a load of towels.

For a second, Drew just watched her. He couldn't help it. She looked so pretty and unguarded. He had thought a lot about their conversation the night before on the patio. In truth, he'd thought about more than just their conversation. He hadn't been able to get her off his mind in general. No matter what he was doing, or whom he was talking to, Whitney was there, in the background of his consciousness. He thought about her smile, her laugh, the way her eyes lit up when she held Elliot for the first time.

She must have realized he was standing there, because she looked up and met his gaze.

"Hi," she said softly before she smiled at him.

His knees went weak and he felt foolish as he grinned back. "Hi."

This was his wife. How was that possible?

He entered the laundry room and took one of the towels to help fold, needing to do something other than stare at her. "How was your day?"

She glanced at the ever-present monitor on the shelf and a tender look crossed her face. "It was hard—but really good. I've never felt more purposeful or fulfilled before in my life."

"You don't mind taking care of Elliot on your own?"

Whitney shook her head, her blond ponytail coming to rest over her shoulder. "I wasn't on my own. Piper stopped by for a few hours to help. She answered all my questions and gave me some tips and tricks—like how not to get peed on again."

Drew made a face. "Did he—?"

"Yes." She laughed. "He did."

Drew laughed, too.

They finished up the towels and Drew took a stack to put away. "Should we order out tonight?"

"Piper brought us lasagna."

"That was really nice."

"And she organized a meal train for the next two weeks from Timber Falls Community Church. She said that Sam and Cricket attended there."

Drew nodded. "I do, too." He hadn't broached the subject of church with her yet. But now seemed like a good time. "Would you like to attend with me on Sunday?"

If Drew remembered correctly, the Emmerson family hadn't been big churchgoers. Cricket had started to attend with Sam, and her parents had come once in a while when they were visiting. But they hadn't raised their daughters in church.

Whitney nibbled her bottom lip for a second. "They are going to a lot of trouble to bring us meals. The least I could do would be to attend the service to thank them."

Drew nodded, happy with her decision. He hoped that once she attended, and she realized what a great group of people she would meet there, she'd want to return with him.

Because more than anything, Drew wanted to raise Elliot with a strong church family.

Not only would it mean a lot to him, it would have meant a lot to Sam and Cricket.

It was just one of many things he was starting to dream about—with Whitney and Elliot at the center of those dreams.

Chapter Six

"I keep wondering how much time we have before he wakes up again," Whitney said a couple hours later while she and Drew ate at the table in the kitchen alcove. They had both agreed that the dining room felt too big and impersonal to eat supper with just the two of them.

"How long was he sleeping before I got home?" Drew asked.

"About thirty minutes." Whitney took a sip of her lemonade, feeling full and satisfied from the lasagna they had just enjoyed. "I imagine he'll be hungry soon. He ate every few hours today. It's incredible! I had no idea a baby ate that much."

Drew smiled at her as he pushed his plate away and leaned back in his seat. "The lasagna was excellent. I'll have to text Piper and thank her for the meal."

Whitney was thankful for more than the meal. Piper's advice and help had been priceless today, but her friendship had been even more of a blessing. They had talked about almost everything. It had been a long time since Whitney had connected with a stranger so quickly. She looked forward to building a friendship with Piper, who had reiterated her desire to help whenever needed. Piper's daughter, Lainey, was a year and a half and Piper had confided that another little Evans baby was on the way.

"She was invaluable to me today." Whitney couldn't hide the appreciation from her voice. "Even though I'm tired, I feel more prepared to care for Elliot—though I have a lot more to learn."

"I'll take nighttime duty tonight, to let you sleep."

She shook her head. "No—you left the house at five fifteen this morning. I'm not going to let you get up with Elliot tonight. I can sleep when he takes his morning nap. You can't."

"I'm happy to do it, Whitney." He watched her, his blue eyes so attractive, she could hardly look at him. "We're a team and I won't let you down."

She couldn't help but smile. "Just having your reassurance is enough. If I need help, I'll be sure to ask for it. You have enough on your plate losing Sam's help from the course."

He looked down at the table and toyed with his napkin. "It's still impossible to believe he's gone."

Whitney nodded. "I haven't had time to really process it yet. I'll need to go through my parents' things at some point—and I'm sure there's a will or something I'll need to deal with."

Drew crossed his arms, but didn't meet her gaze. "I've already been in contact with their lawyer." He paused and glanced up at her. "Apparently, they left everything to Cricket and her descendants."

A lump formed in Whitney's throat. "I wasn't even mentioned?" She didn't want their possessions or their money, but being left out of their will felt like the final thread that had held them together was severed.

Drew shook his head. "I'm sorry, Whitney. It will all be rolled into Elliot's trust."

She lifted a shoulder, feeling a bit numb. "I don't need any of it—and frankly, I'm not surprised."

He leaned forward, his gaze penetrating hers. "What happened between you? What could have possibly been so bad that you left and never spoke to them again?"

"My mom wanted it that way. Said I had ruined everything."

"What did you do?"

"I was born."

He stared at her, a frown marring his handsome face.

"I know that sounds melodramatic, but it's true," she said.

He already knew that she had given up her dream to be a music teacher and start her own school—why not tell him everything? Get it out in the open. He'd probably find out anyway, and the sooner he knew who she really was, the better.

"Ever since I was little," she began, trying to decide how best to tell him, "I knew that I wasn't wanted. My parents made it clear—and it became worse when they realized I didn't fit in with them." The chair she was sitting on suddenly felt uncomfortable—or maybe it was how closely he studied her. Either way, she felt like squirming, but refrained. "I learned when I was about ten that my mom and dad had wanted only one child, and they had her—Cricket. Apparently, my mom suffered postpartum depression so badly after Cricket was born that she was terrified to have more children, so my father had a surgical procedure to prevent another pregnancy. My mom was just starting to feel better when they discovered she was pregnant with me."

"How was that possible?"

Whitney shrugged. "Something went wrong with his procedure. My mom plunged back into depression and my dad blamed the pregnancy—and ultimately, me. She struggled with something called postpartum psychosis after I was born, and she was hospitalized for a long time. I don't have many memories of her from my early years."

She thought about the dark, quiet house, the extended family who came over often to check on them when her dad was at work, and visiting her mom at the hospital a few hours away when she was at her worst.

"I never felt like my mom or dad forgave me," she continued. "The older I got, and the more I didn't conform to their expectations, the more they disliked me. Any time my mom went into a bout of depression, it was usually linked back to me somehow. A bad report card, some sort of behavior issue, or a failure."

Whitney still felt the weight of that responsibility on her shoulders. She had been tainted before birth, completely unwanted. Her life had been one big disappointment after another.

The table was small and Drew was close enough to reach across the space and take her hand in his. "I'm sorry, Whitney. None of that is your fault, you know that, right?"

His hand was warm and gentle, and his words, though reassuring, didn't reach the depth of her pain.

"As an adult, I recognize that I couldn't possibly be at fault," she acknowledged. "But as a child, it wasn't that easy to understand and there was a lot of hurt and damage done very early on." The fears and lies taunted her all the time. What if she *was* a mistake? What if God didn't truly want her, either?

"What happened at Cricket's wedding?"

Drew asked, letting her hand go. Had he even realized he'd reached for her? It had seemed so natural. Instinctual.

This was one of the harder parts of the story to tell and Whitney had to take a deep breath before she began. "My parents never wanted me to teach music. They had aspirations for me to be a lawyer or doctor or engineer, or something that made a lot of money. I had no desire to even go to college, because I just wanted to offer music lessons, but they didn't give me much choice. When they realized I wasn't going to pursue a career they liked, they said they didn't care where I went, or what I studied, but I had to go to college. So I attended Berklee College of Music in Boston and graduated the summer that Cricket and Sam got married."

She had wanted desperately to prove herself to her parents that summer. She wanted them to know what her professors and classmates had told her over and over—that she was a talented musician and singer. And she was gifted to teach others.

"Cricket told me that there was going to be a music professor at the wedding from the University of Minnesota—" Whitney paused and focused on Drew, realizing the connection. "Apparently, he was a family friend of the Keelans."

Drew nodded. "Kind of a relative, actually. He's married to my cousin."

"Cricket believed in my dream, so— despite my parents' protests—she asked me to sing for their wedding. She said that the professor had connections and it would be a good place for me to start pursuing my dream to teach."

This time, Drew looked down at the table, nodding slowly. Of course he'd have to remember what happened after that. He'd been there. He saw Whitney's big failure.

"I made a mess of the whole wedding," Whitney said quietly. "I was so determined to make my parents proud—and to impress the professor—that I couldn't stand up under the pressure. I panicked and choked."

"You didn't ruin the whole wedding."

"Maybe not the whole thing—but I mortified my parents and Cricket. She was upset with me because I had blown the opportunity she'd given me. At the time, I thought I had embarrassed her, but now I realize I had disappointed her." Whitney let out a sigh. "My parents were furious with me. They accused me of doing it on purpose, that I'd always been jealous of Cricket and I had tried to ruin her wedding. My mom said she'd never forgive me, even though I swore I hadn't done it on purpose. Looking back, I should have been more aware of her mental health. She was stressed out from the wedding and she never did well with stress."

Whitney paused, having a hard time reliving the experience.

"The fight got so out of hand," she continued. "My mother began weeping like I hadn't seen her weep since I was young, and my father was beside himself trying to calm her. He told me that I was a disappointment to them, had been from the moment they learned I was on the way. I said something stupid like, maybe I should never have been born, and he told me that their life would have been a lot easier if I hadn't been."

She pressed her lips together, trying to hold in the tears. The whole thing had been blown out of proportion. Looking back, Whitney knew it was more about the past and less about the actual wedding. For the first time in her life, Whitney had finally confronted her parents with all her hurt and it had not gone well. They never saw their part in her pain.

"I left that night and flew out to stay with my friend in DC. I waited for my parents to contact me, to apologize—but they never did."

Drew's face revealed his shock. Even to Whitney's ears it sounded horrible—and it had been. She'd been hurt, humiliated and ashamed. The rejection she'd felt at her father's words still stung like a fresh wound.

"I'm sorry, Whitney. If it's any consolation, Cricket never once mentioned the wedding or why you left. She always spoke highly of you."

"She must have thought enough about me to name me as Elliot's guardian." Whitney had already taken a measure of comfort in that.

"I know she loved you." Drew offered a tender smile. "And for what it's worth, all I remember from you singing at the wedding is how pretty you looked in your bridesmaid's dress—and how the sun made your hair shimmer like gold."

His unexpected compliment surprised her and her cheeks grew warm. "Thank you," she managed to say, trying not to let his words mean more than they should.

He smiled and then took her plate and

stacked it on his, appearing to make himself busy to avoid the awkward moment.

After a few seconds, he finally looked at her, and she could see that the compliment had been real. Had he found her attractive back then? Did he still find her attractive now?

"I know how you feel," he said, "I regret the last thing I said to my dad. I knew he was sick, but I didn't think it would be our last conversation. I can't even remember why we were fighting. It was something to do with the way I was running the golf course." He shrugged, though Whitney could tell it was still heavy on his heart. "I told him the only reason I was running the course was because he was sick and I didn't have a choice. I then told him that it was his fault I'd given up on my dream to be a professional golfer and that I regretted sacrificing everything for him. He told me to get out of his room, so I stormed off. A few hours later, Sam called to tell me Dad had passed away suddenly, and to this day, I blame myself."

"He had been sick for years, Drew." Whitney shook her head. "I remember Cricket telling me that they had been surprised he lived for so long. It wasn't your fault he died."

"Some days, I believe it," he said. "But most days, I know the truth. I made him so upset it was too much for his frail health. I ultimately killed him." He studied her again, this time his eyes looking more vulnerable than ever. "I've never told anyone about that fight before. Not even Sam."

It was her turn to take his hand in hers. "You can trust me."

He nodded. "I know."

In some ways, Whitney felt like she'd unloaded a heavy burden. In other ways, she was weighed down more than ever before.

But it was good to know she wasn't alone.

* * *

The hot shower had felt good, but it made Drew even more tired than he'd been before. It was only eight o'clock, but getting up at four thirty made for a long day. Especially after all the work at the course and the emotional conversation he'd had after supper with Whitney.

He pulled on a T-shirt and ran the comb through his hair as he looked at his reflection in the foggy bathroom mirror. He'd never thought he'd tell anyone about his last conversation with his dad, but it had come so easily tonight. He had *wanted* to tell Whitney. Sharing the truth with her had freed him like nothing ever had. He knew exactly what she was going through with the unresolved grief after losing her family, though, in his mind, she wasn't at fault—not like he had been. Whitney's family had wrongfully accused her all her life and it seemed that nothing she could do would bring her out from the stigma of her birth.

It broke his heart.

He, on the other hand, had made the choice to accuse his dad of ruining his life. At the time, he knew it wasn't true, but he'd been angry. He just wished he'd had a chance to apologize and tell his dad that it had been his own choice to leave competitive golf.

Turning off the light, Drew left his bathroom and heard the faint sound of a song.

He exited his room and followed the singing to the nursery, where the door was cracked open.

Whitney was sitting on the rocking chair with Elliot in her arms. The baby was looking up at her as he drank from his bottle—and Whitney was singing a song he didn't recognize, though it was the most beautiful sound he'd ever heard.

As she sang, she ran her finger over Elliot's cheek.

The scene stopped him in his tracks, filling his heart to the brim.

There was not one thing wrong with Whitney—despite what her parents had said. Though he recognized some of her insecurities, and shared a few, he saw nothing but kindness, beauty and sacrifice in her every move. Just like him, she was searching for her place in the world and he hoped and prayed they had both found it.

His attraction for her stirred. He couldn't help thinking about holding her hand earlier and telling her how beautiful she had been at the wedding. Yet, he couldn't let his attraction grow. Theirs was not a love match. They were friends, co-parents and managers of Elliot's future. That was all. To risk anything more was not worth the inevitable pain. If Whitney fell in love with someone else, he had promised to let her out of the marriage, and he would keep his word, no matter how much it hurt. It would be better to not lose his heart to her in the process.

He pushed the door open and Whitney looked up at him, the song dying on her lips.

"Don't stop," he said quietly as he entered the nursery.

She took the bottle from Elliot and put him up to the burp cloth on her shoulder. "Piper told me we have to burp him after every couple of ounces."

"What were you singing?" He wouldn't let her change the subject.

"It was nothing. Just something I wrote."

"It was incredible, Whitney." He took a seat on the footstool near the crib, realizing he might be making her uncomfortable in his pajamas. But living together was bound to bring them into intimate situations. Might as well get used to it now.

"Thank you." She patted Elliot's back gently.

"I didn't know you were a songwriter, too."

She shrugged. "I just dabble at it."

"You should do it more often." He had intended to talk to her about something earlier, but it hadn't come up—and with the seriousness of their after-supper conversation, it hadn't felt like a good time. "I wanted to run an idea by you, but don't feel obligated to say yes."

"I'm happy to help. What do you need?"

The stool wasn't comfortable, but he didn't want to stand above her as he asked her. "I told you that we're hosting a PGA qualifying event at the course in a couple of weeks."

She nodded and got Elliot to burp. Slowly, she laid him back in her arms to continue feeding him.

"Among other things, we're in charge of the evening entertainment." He wasn't sure how she'd feel about this request. "I was wondering if you'd consider singing for us."

Whitney stared at him for a few moments, though it felt like much longer. "I don't know, Drew. I think you could find someone more qualified."

"I don't think so." He leaned forward.

"You're extremely talented—and hearing you just now confirms what I've always known." He smiled. "What good is marriage if it doesn't make us better people? I want you to reach your potential, and if I can help in any way, I want to. I'd love for you to sing for us."

"What about *your* potential?" she asked. "Are you competing in the event?"

He looked down at his hands and shook his head. "I have too much to do that day."

"Can't someone else do it? Just this once? You'd have home field advantage— wouldn't you?"

"I don't know, Whitney." He had been trying to convince himself for months of all the reasons he shouldn't enter.

"I'll make a deal with you," she said quietly, bringing his gaze back up to hers. "If you compete in the tournament, I'll sing that evening."

For a long time, he didn't say anything. Dozens of arguments cropped up in his mind, but he knew she'd have an answer for all of them. There really was no logical reason why he shouldn't compete.

"If nothing else," she said, "do it for Sam and your dad. See what happens— take a risk with your dream."

He took a deep breath. "Are you truly willing to do the same thing? What if I can get my cousin's husband to come to the event? Would you be willing to sing for him? I'm sure he still has connections. It's not too late for you to pursue your dream to teach again. Maybe even at a college level."

It was her turn to hesitate, and he could see lots of arguments coming to her mind, too.

"Sure." It was all she said.

He lifted his eyebrows, incredulous. "You'll do it?"

"I will if you will."

A smile broke out on Drew's face. "Okay. You have yourself a deal." He stood and offered his hand. She reached out and shook it.

Something powerful passed between them, but Drew didn't know if it was attraction or a shared goal. Whatever it was, it was becoming more and more difficult to ignore.

Chapter Seven

It was a week since Whitney had arrived
in Timber Falls and six days since she'd
married Drew. In that short week, she'd
begun to feel as if she'd never known any
other way of life. Her work at the Hard
Rock Cafe felt like a distant dream—one
she was happy she'd woken up from. Her
landlady had shipped her few belongings
to Timber Falls and donated the larger
items, like her furniture, to Goodwill.

Whitney no longer had connections or
ties to Washington, DC. And despite her
responsibility to Elliot, and the long hours

and late nights, she had never felt happier in her life.

She loved being his caregiver and sharing her life with Drew.

Yet, there was a part of her that felt like a failure. She'd graduated from college four years ago, with a prestigious degree from Berklee, and she had nothing to show for it. She had thought a lot about Drew's request to sing for his event, and though she'd told him she would, there was a part of her that wondered if she would choke up again. Could she actually do it, especially if there was a music professor in the audience? The same one that had watched her fail miserably four years ago?

Singing professionally wasn't her dream, but it was all connected. If she couldn't perform in front of people, how in the world was she going to teach others to do that very thing?

The sun was bright in the afternoon sky as Whitney pushed Elliot in his stroller toward the golf course. It was the final day the construction workers would be at the house and they no longer needed her input or direction. The interior designer, Liv Harris, was there with a team of her decorators putting the house together per Cricket's instructions. Whitney trusted Liv to make it look beautiful, and more importantly, she still felt like a guest in Cricket and Sam's house. She didn't think she should have a say in how things were decorated. If she stayed home, then Liv would ask for her input and Whitney wasn't ready to give it.

One day, perhaps, it would feel like home. But not yet. Right now her only concern was caring for Elliot.

The baby soon fell asleep as Whitney pushed him along the cart path. The grass was lush green, the flowers were beautiful, and singing birds flitted through the tall trees. Golfers walked by or drove their carts, though no one seemed to be in a hurry.

She'd forgotten how relaxing it could be

on the golf course. Good memories of her days working the beverage cart returned, filling her with an unexpected happiness. Not all her childhood memories were bad, especially after she'd gotten to high school and had her own driver's license. She was able to go where she wanted and do what she wanted. It had actually been hard sometimes, though, that her parents didn't care too much about where she was, or who she was with. As long as she didn't embarrass them or get caught doing something she shouldn't.

Which she never had. Whitney hadn't been one to get into trouble. In her mind, there was no point. It wasn't worth the inevitable ugliness that would follow at home.

It took a while to walk across the expanse of the course. She had decided to surprise Drew and his staff with a visit from Elliot, since he had mentioned that several people were asking how the baby was doing. The employees were like family and they'd be interested in watching Sam and Cricket's son grow up. And it would be good for Elliot to be exposed to the golf course as often as possible, since it was part of his family's legacy and would be his one day, if he wanted it.

As she got closer to the clubhouse, she glanced at the driving range and spotted a familiar figure.

Drew.

He was standing with about a dozen children of elementary school age, watching as they practiced their golf swings. He was wearing his typical attire—a pair of dark, tailored trousers and a long-sleeved golfing shirt. His torso was slim and his shoulders were well formed from all his years of golfing.

She almost paused to admire him, but didn't want to get caught gawking. Instead, she approached the driving range from behind the students, who were clearly in the middle of a lesson.

"Jordan, pull up a little on your club,"

Drew said to one of the boys. "Straighten out your elbows and keep your eye on the ball."

"Got it, Coach!" Jordan said with a big grin as he repositioned his stance and then swung at the ball again. This time, it flew straight. "Yes!"

"All right!" Drew gave the boy a high five. "That's what I'm talking about. Do that every time and you'll be playing professional before you know it."

Drew walked up and down the line, giving a tip here, a pointer there, and an encouraging word to almost each child.

It warmed Whitney's heart to see him investing in a younger generation. He was busy, running the course without Sam's help, but he was still taking time to coach the kids.

There were a couple of high school students helping, so when Drew turned at Whitney's arrival, he was able to jog away from the kids and meet her on the cart path.

"Whitney!" He grinned, his eyes lighting up with pleasure at her unexpected visit. "What are you doing here?"

"I thought Elliot and I would come for a visit. You mentioned that the staff were asking about him."

His grin widened. "They'll be thrilled to see you both." He motioned to the kids. "I'm just about ready to wrap up here. Let me give my assistants a couple of notes and I'll walk you into the clubhouse."

Whitney nodded and watched him jog back to the kids.

"Is that your girlfriend?" Jordan asked, a gleam in his eye.

Drew turned to look back at Whitney and winked at her. "Nope. That's my wife."

"Your *wife*!" said another kid.

"Yep." Drew put his hand on the boy's shoulder and turned him back to his golf clubs. He looked at his watch. "You have about ten minutes until your parents will be here to pick you up. Take a few more swings and then head out to the range to pick up your balls."

He gave a few more instructions to his teen helpers and then rejoined Whitney.

"You didn't need to leave early on our account," Whitney said as they started to walk toward the clubhouse. "I would have happily watched you work."

He glanced at her, a smile on his handsome face. Something about the way he looked at her—and the way he'd winked earlier—made her cheeks grow warm.

"You're welcome to come anytime—to watch me work." He winked again, but this time, Whitney shook her head and teasingly rolled her eyes.

"Really," he said as he grew a little more serious. "I'd love to take you out golfing some time. Maybe we can get a babysitter for Elliot and play a few holes."

She looked down at the tiny little boy. He had just turned a month old the day before. "Do you think he's ready for a babysitter?"

"I think the better question to ask is whether or not *you're* ready for him to have a babysitter."

"Touché." She laughed.

"Before I forget," Drew said as they crossed the parking lot near the clubhouse, "I got a phone call about an hour ago from our next-door neighbors, the Johnsons. Mrs. Johnson is scheduled to bring supper to us tonight, but she asked if we'd like to go to their house, instead. Their daughter, Adley, and son-in-law, Nate, will be there and they thought you might like to meet them. They weren't in church last week."

"That's kind of them." Whitney had met Rick and Susan Johnson—and many other people—when they'd gone to church on Sunday. Several people were already familiar to her, since they'd been coming by with meals every night—and because Whitney had grown up in Timber Falls. But there were new people, too, like Adley and Nate.

"They asked us to stop by around five."

Drew held the clubhouse door open for Whitney. "It doesn't give us much time, but does that work for you?"

Whitney shrugged. "Ask my social secretary." She motioned to Elliot. "He usually dictates my schedule."

Drew grinned and nodded. "Hopefully he'll be amenable to the idea."

They entered the clubhouse and Elliot was a huge hit. Everyone from the clubhouse pro to the gift shop manager came to admire the baby.

And despite his adoring crowd, he slept through the whole event.

It wasn't until Whitney was about to leave that Heather appeared from around a corner. She had somehow not received the memo that Elliot had come to visit— or she had chosen to ignore their presence. Regardless, she seemed surprised to find Whitney and Elliot standing there in the entrance lobby.

The other staff members had returned to their duties, and Drew had gone to his office to grab his cell phone since it was after four and he planned to go home with Whitney and Elliot.

Whitney and Heather hadn't seen each other since the wedding day, and though Drew rarely mentioned Heather, she was often on Whitney's mind. How could she not be? She worked with Drew every day, and given their past history, Whitney often wondered if Drew regretted marrying her and not Heather. Drew and Heather clearly had a lot in common, and there must have been some kind of attraction between them if they had gone out a few times.

"Hello," Whitney said, forcing herself to smile.

"Oh," Heather said, "are you still here? I thought you'd be long gone by now."

The way she said it made Whitney wonder if she meant long gone from Timber Falls—as if it was common for Whitney to run off.

"No," Whitney said, feeling less capable of maintaining her smile. "I'm still here."

Heather's smile seemed just as forced as Whitney's. She looked down at Elliot and her entire face transformed. "Look at him! He's adorable."

Whitney was thankful for the baby's presence to ease the tension.

"How old is he now?" Heather asked. "A month? I bet he's awake more during the day, drinking a few more ounces of formula and becoming a little more alert."

"He is." Whitney was surprised that she'd know so much about a one-month-old, but then again, why wouldn't she?

"I used to be a nanny," Heather said, as if to answer Whitney's unasked question. "I love babies. I used to think I would have a houseful of them one day."

Whitney didn't know what to say to that. Drew appeared just then.

"He's so cute," Heather said to Drew. "How can you stand to leave him all day?"

"It's not easy," Drew acknowledged.

"If you ever need a babysitter," Heather said to Drew, "don't hesitate to ask me. I'd love to sit with him."

Drew's face lit up. "Actually—"

"Thank you for the offer," Whitney interrupted him. "If we need a sitter, we'll let you know." She looked to Drew. "We should probably head back. He's due for another feeding soon and we need to get to our neighbors for supper."

Drew nodded and opened the door for Whitney to push the stroller through.

"Bye," Whitney said to Heather as she hurried out of the clubhouse.

She didn't know why, but she didn't like that Heather seemed so...capable.

The Johnsons' home was beautiful and smelled of beef stew and corn bread. Drew sat in the formal dining room with Whitney at his side and Elliot in his right arm. Every little detail was picture-perfect and there wasn't a single item out of place. To Drew, the house felt like a throwback to a

1950s' sitcom. He half expected to see a TV mom pop out of the kitchen in a dress and apron with a big smile on her face— though Susan Johnson was as close to a 50s housewife as Drew could imagine, with her perfectly styled hair and freshly pressed clothing.

"Thank you so much for inviting us," Whitney said as she sat at the table next to Drew. She looked afraid to touch anything, and he didn't blame her. There were two forks to the left of the gold-rimmed plates, a knife and spoon to the right and a dessert fork at the top. Folded linen napkins sat atop the plates like little hats, and crystal goblets were poised to accept whatever refreshment Mrs. Johnson would serve.

"It's our pleasure," Mrs. Johnson said as she touched Whitney's shoulder while setting a bread basket on the table.

"I wish you'd let me help you," Whitney said, attempting to rise.

Mrs. Johnson kept her hand on Whitney's shoulder. "You stay put. I'm all alone in this big old house, practically at my leisure, while you've been caring for that precious baby all week. This is my treat to you. Rest and relax."

Whitney looked to Drew, as if for help, but all he could do was smile. He agreed with Mrs. Johnson. Whitney had been working hard and she deserved a break.

"I don't know what could be keeping Adley and Nate," Mr. Johnson said as he glanced at his watch for the third time since they sat down. "They're usually so punctual."

"Beekeeping is a hard job," Mrs. Johnson said to her husband as she took a seat at the foot of the table, closest to the kitchen door. "They'll be along shortly."

"I gave Adley a hundred reasons why it was a bad idea to keep bees," Mr. Johnson said as he leaned back in his chair and folded his arms. "But would she listen to me? Nate could have come to work with me at the bank, but neither one of them has much sense."

"Oh, hush," said Mrs. Johnson to her husband as she looked at Whitney and smiled. "I think you'll like our Adley. She and Nate were married last fall, but they'd been friends since they were children. Adley's first husband, Benjamin, died while he was deployed in Afghanistan, and Nate was his best friend. Nate came back to Timber Falls to help Adley run the bee farm and they fell madly in love." She sighed. "We couldn't be happier."

"I could be happier," Mr. Johnson said under his breath. "Where are they?"

Mrs. Johnson gave her husband a look, but then smiled again at Whitney and Drew. "Now, tell me about your love story."

Whitney quickly glanced at Drew. He could see panic in her eyes. "We—we—"

"We're enjoying being newlyweds," Drew said as he gently took Whitney's hand in his own, not wanting her to feel like she had to explain anything. Their marriage was their business, and if she didn't want others to know the details, then she didn't need to share. There were people who would probably assume it was a marriage of convenience, but not everyone would know. "I couldn't be happier."

Whitney looked down at his hand, and he belatedly realized he'd done it again. He had taken her hand on instinct, without even realizing what he was doing. It felt like the most natural thing in the world, though he hadn't asked her and didn't know if she wanted him to hold her hand or not.

So he let it go.

"I'm sure you were so thankful that Whitney agreed to a quick wedding," Mrs. Johnson continued. "I know how most women long for a proper church wedding with all her friends and family nearby—but a woman who would give all that up to focus on taking care of the baby is a real gem, Drew."

"I couldn't agree more." Drew *did* know how blessed he was that Whitney had agreed to a quick wedding. But what if Mrs. Johnson was right? Did Whitney want a big church wedding with all her friends and whatever family they had left? Had he somehow deprived her of a dream? He wanted to ask her, but they were interrupted.

"Hello," a woman called out from the front entry. "Sorry we're late."

"That's my Adley," Mrs. Johnson said with excitement as she stood and scurried out of the dining room. "She'll have Benny with her, too. He's fifteen months old and quite a handful at the moment."

"Benny is Adley's son with her first husband," Mr. Johnson explained, though for Whitney's benefit, no doubt. Drew had known the Johnsons almost all his life. He was very familiar with Adley's story. He even knew Nate, though they hadn't been in the same friend group in high school. "Adley's first husband was a beekeeper, but she inherited the farm when he passed away. After she married Nate, they decided to stay on."

Whitney nodded her understanding, making Drew wish he had thought to explain the situation to her before they came over to the Johnsons'.

A few moments later, Mrs. Johnson returned to the dining room holding her grandson, with Adley and Nate walking close behind her.

Adley was medium height, with soft brown hair and sparkling green eyes. She had a spray of freckles across her nose and pretty features. Nate was tall and well-built, carrying himself with a military bearing. His dark hair was cut short and his skin was tan, no doubt from being outside all spring with their bees.

Benny looked a lot like his mama.

"Hello," Adley said. "I'm sorry we're late. Grandpa Jed's arthritis flared up this afternoon and I needed to get him settled into his favorite recliner with a TV dinner before we could leave."

"Grandpa Jed is Adley's grandfather through marriage," Mrs. Johnson said in her congenial voice. "He was really Benjamin's grandpa, but he lives with them on the farm."

"That's nice," Whitney said.

Introductions were made and then Adley and Nate Marshall took their seats across from Whitney and Drew. Mrs. Johnson put Benny in a high chair and Mr. Johnson said a blessing over the meal before Mrs. Johnson took the lid off the soup tureen.

"I hope you like homemade beef stew and fresh-baked cornbread," Mrs. Johnson said to Whitney.

"I love it." Whitney smiled at their hostess. "It's been years since I've had any, but my mouth is already watering."

"Oh, good."

"We are so sorry for your loss," Adley said to Whitney and Drew, her green eyes filled with compassion. "If there's anything we can do to help, please let us know. And I mean it."

"We appreciate that," Drew said as he gently set Elliot into his car seat so he could eat his beef stew without spilling it on his nephew.

"Everyone has been amazing," Whitney said. "We really appreciate the nightly meals. They help more than anyone could know."

"The church did the same for me after Benny was born and it was a lifesaver." Adley dipped her spoon into her stew. "A warm meal goes a long way in blessing someone when they adjust to having an infant to care for."

As the meal progressed, Drew couldn't help noticing how Nate drew his chair up a little closer to Adley, and how the two of them glanced at each other, love and a bit of wonder in their gazes. At one point, during dessert, Nate took Adley's hand and held it for the rest of the meal.

They laughed at each other's jokes, exchanged knowing smiles, and when Adley's dad seemed bent on giving them a hard time about their bee farm, they stood as a united front against his pesky comments.

They were in love and it was heartwarming to witness, though it made Drew feel less and less married by the second. Yes, he and Whitney were married—in the eyes of the law. But was that truly enough? He considered his own parents' happy marriage. They'd been together for twenty-three years before Drew's mom died of breast cancer. It had destroyed his dad and he'd never fully recovered. His health had faded little by little over the years, until the doctors had diagnosed him with multiple sclerosis. He'd refused any kind of aggressive treatment that might have offered him a few more years. One of Dad's doctors had been real with Sam and Drew and told them that the will to live was one of the most powerful medicines on the planet—but Dad didn't have that will. He faded quickly and once they had the diagnosis, he went fast.

Romantic love was a gift from God—one that Drew and Whitney did not share. For now, they both seemed okay with it, but how long would that last? Drew could see how Whitney watched Adley and Nate. How much time did they have before one or both of them grew bitter or disillusioned with their situation? Before the reality of their marriage was too much for them to accept?

In that moment, Drew realized he knew nothing about Whitney's love life. Had she ever been in a serious relationship? Had she been hurt?

The thought of another man hurting her gave Drew the strangest sensation he'd ever felt. His emotions were strong and overpowering, but he had nowhere to direct his anger or resentment.

As they wrapped up the evening and

prepared to walk home, all Drew could think about was whether or not someone had hurt Whitney.

Chapter Eight

It was still light out as Whitney and Drew left the Johnsons' house after supper. The sun wouldn't set until after eight, so they had another hour to enjoy the daylight.

The houses were impressive and the yards were large, making the houses farther apart than most neighborhoods. Whitney loved the privacy it afforded, especially with the river on the back of Cricket and Sam's property. Though they were close to town, it felt like they were a world apart from the busyness of Main Street. It was definitely a change from Washington, DC.

"I'm full," Whitney said as she sighed with contentment. "Mrs. Johnson is a great cook. I just wish she would have let me help with the dishes."

Drew pushed the stroller along the road, and for the first time since they'd been married, he wasn't fully present for their conversation. All throughout supper, he had grown quieter and quieter, and now his mind seemed far off. He didn't answer her, appearing not to have heard her, or thought her statement was worth commenting on.

Whitney glanced away from him, wondering what had caused him to retreat into his own mind. Was it something she had said or done? She tried thinking back to when she noticed him withdrawing, but she couldn't remember anything she might have said to upset him.

They walked for a few minutes in silence, each in their own thoughts.

The Marshalls had been a fun couple and Whitney was excited to get to know them better. Yet, watching them had been difficult. They were clearly in love—and for all intents and purposes, they were the newlyweds, not Whitney and Drew. Being married was something so much more than signing a marriage certificate. It was the coming together of two lives to make one—in spirit, body and soul. Drew and Whitney had come together to raise their nephew—had signed the dotted line—but they weren't married in that true sense of the word.

Though Whitney hated to admit it to herself, she was envious of the Marshalls' relationship. Of their happiness, their togetherness.

"Have you ever been in love, Whitney?" Drew asked quietly.

His question pulled Whitney out of her reverie, startling her with its suddenness.

"What?" she asked, though she had heard him perfectly.

He continued to push Elliot, but he

looked up and met her gaze. "Have you ever been in love?"

She focused on the road ahead, wondering why her heart beat so hard at his question. Shadows filtered through the tiny leaves on the trees as she pondered why he would ask her that question right now, and how she should answer.

"Yes," she finally said, though she hated to admit that she had given her heart to an untrustworthy man.

If she wasn't mistaken, Drew's knuckles turned white as he gripped the handle of the stroller—though why, she couldn't be sure.

"His name is Brock Crockett," Whitney said quietly, carefully, waiting for his response. Surely he knew the name?

Drew came to a stop. "Brock Crockett, the musician?"

She also stopped walking. "Have you heard of him?"

"Of course I've heard of him—who

hasn't? Didn't he win a Grammy last year for Best New Artist?"

Whitney looked away from Drew, hoping that he couldn't see the contents of her heart right now. A part of her was happy for Brock—he had achieved what he wanted. Yet, he'd hurt her. He'd chosen his career over their relationship, and worse, he hadn't asked her to be a part of his dream.

"He did win Best New Artist last year," Whitney finally said.

"And you dated him?" Drew's voice was incredulous.

She just shrugged and then continued to walk. "We met soon after I started working at the Hard Rock Cafe in DC. He was working there to save money as he played gigs in the city, trying to get discovered. We hit it off immediately with our mutual love of music."

They had become inseparable from the beginning. The relationship had been intense and all-consuming. Looking back,

Whitney knew it was partially due to her being in a new city, soon after being rejected by her parents. She was lonely and hurting, and Brock was exciting and full of promises. They'd had a few friends in common from Berklee and he'd been in the city for a year, so he knew his way around, making Whitney trust him all the more. He was talented, handsome and confident—and Whitney knew he would go far.

He just went there without her.

"How long were you together?" Drew asked.

"About a year." It had been an intense year full of highs and lows. "When he finally landed his record deal, he moved to Nashville, never looking back. He didn't even ask me if I wanted to follow him and pursue his dream with him. I wasn't good enough for him anymore."

"That can't be true."

"I'm not saying it because I want your pity, or because I feel sorry for myself."

She shrugged. "It's just the way it is. Brock had a dream and I wasn't part of it." The breakup had been just as intense as the relationship had been. They had never done anything without passion—and their final argument had been loud and difficult. At the end, Brock had said the one thing Whitney had hoped and prayed he would not say, the one thing that would silence her for good. He had told her that their relationship had been a mistake.

She had been a mistake. Again.

She tried not to let the hurt penetrate her words as she told Drew about her relationship, but how could it not?

Would Drew look at her one day and tell her that their marriage had been a mistake, too?

She couldn't bear to think about it, because even though she and Drew had not been together long, she already cared far more what he thought of her than anyone else. And it scared her like nothing ever had.

"I'm sorry, Whitney." There was frustration in Drew's voice—frustration and something more. "I hate that he hurt you."

Whitney looked to Drew with surprise. His sincerity was written all over his face.

"I hate that anyone has hurt you," he said, a little quieter.

She looked forward again, trying to understand why he would care so much. "It's okay."

"No." He stopped again, and this time, he turned toward her. "It's not okay."

For some reason, tears gathered in Whitney's eyes at the look of pain on Drew's face. As if he felt the aching in her heart and was carrying the burden with her.

"I know that every coin has two sides," he continued, "and I'm sure there are a lot of things you'd like to redo if given the chance, but you never deserved to be cast aside." He studied her, his blue eyes so full of compassion and understanding she felt as if they were wrapping around her in a tight embrace. "Whether it was your parents—or Brock—or anyone else, you didn't deserve it."

They were standing close—close enough that she could smell the cologne he wore and see the darker flecks of blue in his eyes.

"I can't understand why anyone would choose to walk away from you." His voice was deep and certain.

Warmth filled Whitney's stomach and crept up her chest and neck and into her cheeks. She knew she was blushing and was embarrassed for him to see how his words affected her. She put her hands up to her face and shook her head as she looked away and continued to walk toward the house. "You shouldn't say such things."

"Why not?" he asked gently as he began to push the stroller again. "You're my wife—I should want to be a part of your life, shouldn't I?"

"Yes—but I'm not *really* your wife. Not in the ways that matter." As soon as the words were out of her mouth, she regretted them.

And she could see that Drew regretted them, too.

His lighthearted smile disappeared and he looked out toward the river, his face becoming pensive.

Neither one of them said anything for a few moments, though Whitney tried to find something—anything to break the awkwardness of the moment.

She couldn't think of a thing.

It was Drew who finally found the right words. "We might not be married in *all* the ways that matter, Whitney, but we're married in the ones that matter the most." He stopped again to look at her. "Commitment, sacrifice and trust. And just because we didn't marry for love doesn't mean it's wrong for me to say I want to be a part of your life. Because the more I get to know you, the more it's true. I think you're an amazing woman and I'm honored you're my wife."

She couldn't stop the smile from spreading across her face, even if she had wanted to. "And I'm honored that you're my husband."

He returned her smile and they continued toward the house, turning into the driveway.

A vehicle was parked near the house and when Drew saw it, he groaned.

"What?" Whitney asked.

"It's Kyle and Paula."

The couple must have seen them coming up the driveway, because they got out of their car and turned to face them.

Whitney didn't like that they had come unannounced. "What do you think they want?"

"Knowing Paula? They've come to make trouble."

"What do you think they'd do if we turned around and kept walking?" Whitney asked quietly.

Drew chuckled. "I'd love to see Paula's

face if we did." He sighed. "But, we'll have to face them eventually."

He was right—and there was nowhere to hide.

The last person Drew wanted to see right now was Paula. He was still a little shaken by the knowledge that Whitney's ex-boyfriend was Brock Crockett. The musician had risen in fame over the last two years and was almost always on the radio whenever Drew turned it on.

Now that he knew that Brock had broken Whitney's heart, he'd never admit to her that he had gone to see him in concert when he was in Minneapolis six months ago, or that he was one of Brock's biggest fans.

At least, he used to be. It was one thing to enjoy the man's music, another to know that he had left Whitney after he started rising to fame. There was probably a lot more to the story, and Drew hoped that Whitney would be willing to open up with him about it all one day, but for now, his loyalty to his wife trumped his loyalty to Brock Crockett.

Besides, he had a name and a face to direct the anger he felt to the man who had hurt her—even if it felt a little strange to be upset at a celebrity he admired—used to admire.

But none of that mattered right now. All that mattered was Paula and Kyle standing in his driveway. He hadn't expected to see his cousin again so soon.

"Where were you?" Paula asked when they were close enough to hear her.

"I'm not sure it's any of your business," Drew said as he frowned at her. "What are you doing here, Paula?"

She came up to the stroller, her hands on her hips. "It's too cold and too late to take Elliot on a walk. He shouldn't be out here. He could get sick. What were you two thinking?"

Drew stared at Paula for a heartbeat, too stunned to form a coherent answer.

"It's not that late," Whitney said. "And the air feels wonderful."

"To you, maybe," Paula crossed her arms and stared hard at Whitney. "But babies are different. Their little bodies have a harder time regulating heat. You're up walking around, getting your blood pumping, but he's not moving. He could be freezing to death."

"Paula," Kyle said, a warning in his voice.

Paula didn't seem to notice her husband or care.

"You're not fit to take care of him," Paula said to Whitney. "All you do is think about yourself. That's been your problem since you were little. It's always been about you."

Whitney's lips parted in surprise, but Drew had finally found his voice.

"If you can't speak kindly to my wife," he said, "you need to leave."

"I'm just speaking the truth."

"No." Drew took a step closer to Whitney as he kept one hand on the stroller. "You're throwing verbal mud at her because you're hurt and angry. Elliot is wrapped up in warm clothes, in a warm blanket, cocooned by his car seat. He's happy, healthy and well cared for—because of Whitney's selflessness. She's doing an amazing job."

"And I wasn't? Is that what you're saying, Drew?"

"That's not what he's saying." Kyle came around to his wife. "You need to calm down, Paula. You didn't come here to get into a fight. Tell them what you came to say and then let's go."

Paula's arms were still crossed, but she lifted her chin and seemed to be pulling her emotions together. "I'm not a proud woman."

Drew had to refrain from rolling his eyes. Paula had always been proud.

"So I wanted to let you know that I'm willing to negotiate."

"Negotiate?" Drew frowned. "About what?"

"Elliot."

"There's nothing to negotiate, Paula." Drew gripped the stroller handle, as if Paula was trying to yank it from him.

"The will clearly stated our three names, didn't it?" she asked.

"I suppose."

"Which means that Cricket and Sam wanted the three of us to raise their son."

Drew put up his hand. "That's not what it—"

"More or less," she interrupted him and then she took a deep breath, appearing to try and calm herself. "I know I don't have any legal rights—but I miss him. I love him." She bit her bottom lip and looked toward Kyle, who had compassion in his gaze and nodded for her to continue.

"I'm just asking if I can see him—maybe even on a regular basis," Paula asked. "Like one day a week. That's all I'm asking."

Drew glanced at Whitney, who was looking down at Elliot. He wished he knew what she was thinking.

Granted, he had never gotten along with Paula—but she wasn't a bad person. Just annoying and a bit self-absorbed from time to time. She didn't deserve to have Elliot kept from her forever.

"Whitney and I will talk about it," Drew finally said. "I'll let you know."

"She misses the baby and her best friend," Kyle said to Drew. "She's not asking for much—and it might be a nice break for you two."

Drew nodded absently, though Whitney didn't say a word.

"We should probably get him inside," Drew said. "I'll give you a call tomorrow."

Paula's earlier bluster disappeared and she glanced at the stroller with a look of longing that pierced Drew's heart. Slowly, she bent down and kissed Elliot's forehead.

"Thanks," Kyle said to Drew.

Drew pushed the stroller toward the house with Whitney at his side. Silently, he took the car seat out of the stroller base and they left the base on the porch as they stepped into the house.

Whitney flipped on the light, revealing a home that was completely renovated and redecorated. Gone were the painter's tarps, the sawhorses, the tools and the plastic drapes. Everything looked fresh and new.

"Why does she dislike me so much?" Whitney asked quietly once the front door was closed. "She's always disliked me, ever since I can remember."

"You probably won't like the answer."

Whitney frowned. "No. Probably not."

"It's not because of you." He set the car seat down and walked over to stand in front of her. "Not in the way you think. She doesn't dislike you because there's something wrong with you—she dislikes you because you never bent to her will, and you still don't. I've known Paula all her life and the only people she likes are those she can control. And you, Whitney, are much too self-assured and confident to cow to her whims. That's the only reason she doesn't like you."

She studied him with her brown eyes, so beautiful and uncertain at the moment. He had the sudden desire to take her into his arms and simply hold her. He'd done it once before, the day she had come to Timber Falls. They had shared their sadness and grief, but he wanted to know what it would be like to share happiness and joy in her arms.

The moment grew, swelling with his longing to hold her. Yet, he knew that if he reached for her, she would probably pull away and he would regret placing her in such an awkward position. She had been right. She wasn't his wife in every sense of the word and he didn't have the liberty to touch her and hold her whenever the desire overcame him.

"I should probably make a bottle," she

said, lowering her gaze. "He'll need to be changed and he'll be hungry when he wakes up."

Drew nodded and then left her side to pick up the car seat. "We'll need to talk about Paula's request."

Whitney briefly closed her eyes and then sighed. "Even though we've never gotten along, it wouldn't be right to keep him from her. She *was* Cricket's best friend and she was listed as a possible guardian."

"That's what I was thinking."

"As much as I will hate spending a day without him..." Whitney let the words trail off.

"I'll call them tomorrow and we can work out a day each week for her to spend time with him."

Whitney nodded. "She'll like that."

A gentle smile lifted Drew's lips. He was proud of Whitney, because even though Paula had done nothing kind to her, her heart was big enough to do the right thing.

"What will I do with myself for a whole

day?" Whitney asked, a strange look coming over her face. "And how is it possible that two weeks ago I was living on my own, filling my days and nights with my life—yet, here I am now, wondering what on earth I'll do with a day all to myself."

Drew chuckled, having had the same thought. Two weeks ago, he had been single and on his own, thinking only of himself. But now he was a father and a husband, and he, too, couldn't fathom what they'd do without Elliot for the day.

An idea began to form in his mind and he suddenly knew exactly what they would do.

He just hoped Whitney would like his idea, too.

Chapter Nine

Whitney stood for a minute in the foyer of Cricket's house, absorbing the silence. It was Friday, two days since Paula had shown up and they'd decided to find a day for her to spend with Elliot.

And today was that day. Whitney had just dropped him off for the evening and she was now all alone in the house. Cricket's cleaning service had been there the day before, which meant there were no chores to do. When Whitney had complained to Drew and told him she didn't need a cleaning service, he had told her it wouldn't be right to fire the woman since she'd been working for Cricket for years.

With nothing to occupy her time, Whitney walked into the formal living room and flipped on the light. The room looked like a picture from a magazine and she was almost afraid to sit on the brand-new couch.

Since the US Open qualifying tournament was next Tuesday, Drew was working long days preparing for the event. He had left early that morning and told her he didn't know when he would be home.

It was moments like this when Whitney missed Cricket the most, and when her guilt for how things had ended with her parents threatened to suffocate her. The silence was overwhelming. She and Drew had gone out to see the gravesites and he'd given Whitney the key to her parents' storage unit. But she hadn't had the heart to go through anything yet.

Maybe she couldn't go through the

storage unit, but perhaps her parents' RV would be a better place to start.

Whitney left the living room and walked out the front door. The late afternoon sunshine felt warm on her shoulders. Thankfully, the forecast for the next few days looked to be practically perfect for the tournament.

Though it was warm, Whitney still wrapped her arms around herself as she walked slowly toward the RV. Her parents had bought it the summer she had come home for Cricket's wedding. An aunt and an uncle had used it during the wedding weekend, and then after that, Whitney's mom and dad planned to retire and were going to take it all over the United States. She'd often wondered if they'd come near DC with their RV. She had hoped they would call her one day to say they were in the area, but they hadn't.

The door was unlocked. She pulled it open and the steps extended out automatically.

She'd only been in the RV a couple of times, but it looked like so many others she'd seen. Factory colors, furniture and carpet.

The only thing that set it apart was the smell. Her mom's perfume still lingered, though it had been two and a half weeks since the accident. It almost seemed impossible that it had been so recent. To Whitney's heart and mind, she had lost her parents four years ago. The only difference was that there was no hope of reconciliation now.

Tears gathered in Whitney's eyes as she stood in the vehicle, smelling the musk her mother wore, seeing the reading glasses her father used next to a newspaper that was probably a few weeks old now. There were a couple of cereal bowls in the sink and a towel hanging over the back of a chair. Remnants of her parents' last day before the accident.

Whitney walked toward the back of the RV and what would have been her parents' bedroom. It looked like her mom had recently done some laundry. There was a basket with folded towels sitting on the bed.

Something caught Whitney's eye, lying behind the laundry basket. She walked closer, and as she realized what it was, the tears poured over and trailed down her cheeks.

It was her favorite teddy bear. The one her dad had bought for her on a trip home from visiting her mother in the hospital. She had clung to the bear as a child. There was no mistaking Miss Pretty Bear, as Whitney had called it. A ragged pink bow was stitched next to the ear and one of her button eyes dropped lower than the other, thanks to a family puppy who had thought to make Miss Pretty Bear a chew toy.

A memory surfaced, causing Whitney to sit on the edge of the bed. She lifted Miss Pretty Bear off the pillow and touched that lazy eye.

Whitney had been about eleven—too

old for Miss Pretty Bear to still mean so much, but they had been through a lot together. Her mom was just coming out of one of her episodes and she wanted a puppy. Dad brought one home from a pet shop and they named it Penelope. From the start, Penelope had been more work than Whitney had anticipated. She whined at night, went potty in the house and chewed up everything she could get her paws on—but she made Mom happy.

Penelope had ruined several pairs of shoes and even a book or two before she found Miss Pretty Bear. By the time Whitney had discovered what had happened to her teddy bear, the eyeball was dangling off and Miss Pretty Bear's fur was wet and matted. Whitney had cried so hard she thought her heart would break. Her worst fear was that her mom would tell her to throw out the toy, that she had moved beyond the need for a teddy bear.

But then, her mother had come into the room and when she asked Whitney why she was crying, she had tenderly taken the bear into her arms and looked at the damage Penelope had done. And instead of threatening to throw the toy away, her mom had stopped everything she was doing and had sewn the eye back into place. Then, she had hand-washed Miss Pretty Bear and taken the time to dry her off with a blow dryer.

When Miss Pretty Bear was clean and repaired, her mom had handed the teddy bear back to Whitney and said, "It's the imperfections in each of us that make us unique and special."

Whitney looked at Miss Pretty Bear now, wondering why her parents had kept her childhood toy on their bed. Had it been there since she'd left? And if it had, did it mean that they thought about her? Had wanted something of her to keep close to them?

The bear was a reminder to Whitney that not everything had been hard or un-pleasant growing up. There had been good moments and happy memories among the pain. Miss Pretty Bear was proof.

"Whitney?" Drew's voice called to her from the door of the RV. "Are you in here?"

"I'm here." Whitney laid Miss Pretty Bear back in her place, not wanting to disturb anything. Someday, she'd clean out the RV, but for now, she wanted it to stay just like her parents had left it. In a way, it connected her to them.

She stood as Drew entered the room.

"Are you okay?" he asked, then took a step closer. "Are you crying?"

Whitney wiped at her cheeks and nodded. "Just missing all of them."

"Me, too." He must have noticed the teddy bear, because he said, "Who did that belong to?"

Miss Pretty Bear looked a little pathetic with her wonky eyes, but to Whitney, she was beautiful. "She's mine."

His gaze slipped over to Whitney. "Your parents kept it on their bed?"

"That's what it looks like." Whitney still couldn't believe it. "I don't know if they saved anything else of mine, but to be honest, Miss Pretty Bear is the only thing I would have really missed if they had thrown it away."

"Maybe they saved everything else. There is a pretty large storage shed we need to go through."

She noted how he said *we*, and she liked how it made her feel. Like they were a team and the things that concerned her concerned him. But she didn't want to talk about that right now.

"What brings you home so early?" she asked. "I thought you'd be at the course until this evening."

"I knew you were dropping Elliot off at Paula's and I thought you might like some company."

Warmth filled her chest and she smiled. "You put your work off to keep me company?"

"Not just to keep you company," he

smiled back, his blue eyes crinkling at the corner. "I have an ulterior motive."

"Which is?"

He opened his mouth to respond and then hesitated. Finally he said, "It's a surprise."

"A surprise?"

"Will you come with me?" He offered his hand, palm up. "You deserve a night off."

His hand looked so inviting.

"Okay." She slipped her hand into his warm and strong one.

"Come on." He motioned toward the door with his head. "We have a lot to do tonight."

Whitney couldn't help but smile.

The prospect of spending an entire evening with Drew, with no distractions or responsibilities, made her gloriously excited.

"Don't you have about a thousand things to do before Tuesday?" Whitney asked

Drew as they left Ruby's Bistro after a delicious meal.

Drew wished he had a reason to take Whitney's hand again—even if only for a moment. Leaving her parents' RV with her hand in his had been the highlight of his day.

Up until supper.

Getting to sit across from her, talking to her about everything from childhood memories to current concerns, had been the second highlight.

The third was just around the corner.

"I have the world's best staff," he explained. "And I've worked so hard the past three days that I needed this break as much as you did."

They walked down Main Street, past the shops, the art gallery and the ice cream parlor. The green street lamps were just turning on and there was a hint of light in the western sky. It was Friday night, which meant there was a little extra traffic downtown as people visited the small theater, ate at one of the restaurants or visited the art show at the gallery.

"Is it weird that I miss Elliot and we've only been apart for about three hours?" Whitney asked, turning her dark brown eyes to Drew. She was wearing a simple black dress with a red scarf and a jean jacket. They'd both dressed up a little before leaving home.

His hand accidentally brushed against hers, sending a tingling sensation to the center of his chest. It was one thing to grab her hand to lead her out of a tight spot, but another to openly take her hand on the street for no other purpose than to touch her.

The longing to do that was so powerful it rocked him for a second.

She was watching him for his answer, so he shook his head and smiled. "No. It's not weird at all. It's called love."

"Love is a strange thing, isn't it? The different forms it takes. Until I met Elliot, I never felt this way for anyone in my life. All I want to do is look at him, cuddle him and just be near him." She shook her head in wonder. "And he hasn't done a thing to make me love him, except exist. Being away from him feels like a part of me is missing."

Drew nodded, still trying to understand his own reaction to Whitney. It was almost as if she was explaining his thoughts and feelings toward her. All day, while at work, he couldn't stop thinking about getting home to Whitney. He wanted to be near her, to talk to her, to look at her, to listen to her. And now he had this overwhelming desire to touch her, hold her hand, draw her into his arms.

Was he feeling love? Toward his wife?

The very notion made him pause.

He couldn't fall in love with his wife. It wasn't part of the plan. Just a few weeks ago, he'd hardly known her, and yet, she was almost all he thought about now. But it was more than her just existing. His admiration for her grew in leaps and bounds each day. There were so many things about her that made his heart do funny things whenever he thought about her. The very nature of their relationship had created a bond between them that was unlike any other he'd ever experienced.

But that didn't mean she felt the same way about him. Nothing she had done or said indicated that she reciprocated the warmth of his affections. He couldn't let her know what was on his heart and mind—especially because he hardly understood it himself. They didn't need another complication to worry about.

They walked in silence until they reached the end of the block and then Whitney turned to Drew and said, "Where to next? Are we going home?"

"Not yet." Paula would have Elliot until nine, which meant they still had a couple of hours to spend together. "What do you think about dancing?"

"Dancing?" She lifted her eyebrows. "What kind of dancing?"

"You'll see."

A live orchestra was playing in Maple Island Park near downtown, along the banks of the Mississippi River. The musicians were conducted by one of Drew's longtime employees and friends. They played the second Friday of each month, May through October. It was one of several events that took place at the park.

Drew and Whitney walked down the hill toward the dam that held the waterfall back. It had always been one of his favorite spots in town. A beautiful park ran the length of the river, starting at the dam and winding south toward the Asher property, where a Victorian mansion overlooked the park and the river beyond.

Gentle music drifted on the breeze—following the river on a tender ribbon of sound.

They strolled the cobbled path leading toward the pavilion where the musicians were playing. There were dozens of people dancing under the gazebo-like structure, but they were still far enough away that Drew couldn't make out their faces.

What he could make out was the tune the orchestra had just started. "The Way You Look Tonight" fell off the strings of the instruments, wrapping around Drew.

Whitney began to hum with the tune.

Drew wasn't sure he wanted to try to dance with her under the pavilion, where it was crowded. Maybe here, along the path, where there was no one to bother or distract them, was a better idea.

He stopped and offered his hand. "Will you dance with me, Whitney?"

She stopped humming and looked around them. The river was a stone's throw away to their right and a row of townhouses was across the road to their left. "Here?"

Drew nodded. "I'd rather have you all to myself."

Whitney's smile was shy as she took his hand. "I'd love to."

Slowly, tentatively, she came into his arms. This was much different than the last time he'd held her, when they were both grieving. This time, he was fully conscious of the floral scent of her shampoo, and of the way his pulse thrummed through his veins.

"Some day," Whitney began to sing softly, *"when I'm awfully low, when the world is cold, I will feel a glow just thinking of you, and the way you look tonight."*

He drew her closer and she laid her cheek against his chest as their feet moved along the cobblestone in perfect unison, as if they'd danced together for years.

Whitney's voice was the only sound he heard as she continued singing the song. *"With each word your tenderness grows, tearing my fears apart."*

Drew closed his eyes, his chest expanding with the sound of her voice, the touch of her hand in his, and the power of the song she sang.

The last of the pinks and oranges faded from the sky and the lamppost nearby offered a soft glow on the path. He'd never imagined a moment like this—one so perfect and charming. Until Whitney Emmerson had walked into his life, he hadn't realized what he had been missing or how his heart had longed for another to fill it so completely.

When the last note hummed on the violin string, Whitney finished singing, but neither of them pulled apart.

They came to a stop and Whitney lifted her cheek off Drew's chest, looking up at him with her big brown eyes, so tender and beautiful.

Neither one spoke for a moment. Drew was afraid that if he said something, it would shatter this moment—and he didn't want this to end.

Ever.

"Thank you," Whitney finally whispered. "You're a wonderful dancer."

He wanted to run his finger along her cheekbone to see if her skin was as soft as it looked. But he ran his thumb over the back of her hand, instead.

"I love your voice, Whitney."

She pulled back then, giving them space. Something shifted in her face. "I've been meaning to talk to you about that."

"About your voice?"

"I haven't sung in front of a large crowd since Cricket's wedding and that was a disaster. I—I don't know if I can sing at the country club on Tuesday."

"What?" He frowned.

"I feel too rusty for such an important night. I don't want to ruin anything for you."

"You couldn't ruin anything. Whitney, your voice is amazing." He meant it with all his heart. "You're not rusty at all."

She walked away from him and shook her head. "It's one thing to sing a quiet song or lullaby for an audience of one. Another thing to sing for a crowd. I'd be too nervous to do it again for the first time when it's so important to you."

The orchestra was starting another tune, giving Drew an idea. His employee Ed, who conducted the orchestra, would love to have Whitney join them for a song or two. He was always telling Drew he wished they could find a vocalist to join their group. If Drew asked him, he was certain they'd let her sing tonight.

"Come on," he said, taking her hand again. "I have a great way for you to shake off the rust."

She was hesitant, but she didn't resist him or let go of his hand as he led her to the pavilion.

Chapter Ten

❧

Whitney shook her head as she realized what Drew was suggesting. She pulled on his hand, causing him to stop.

"I can't."

"It's okay. The conductor is a good friend of mine. He'd jump at the chance to have you join them tonight."

"But I don't know him—I haven't had a chance to practice." She swallowed as anxiety tried to creep up her throat. "What if I fail miserably?"

Drew looked deep into Whitney's eyes, captivating all of her senses. "What if you succeed? What if all your dreams come true, Whit?"

The truth hit her between the eyes. "It's almost scarier to think about success than failure. What if my dream comes true and it's nothing like I imagined? What if I hate it—what will I cling to then?"

A gentle breeze ruffled Drew's hair as he said quietly, "Maybe letting go of one dream will allow a new one to be born."

A new dream had already started to grow in Whitney's heart, surprising her with both its tenderness and strength. Whenever her mind used to wander, she would think about owning her own music school, teaching students, sharing her love of music with others. But now, when her mind had a moment to itself, all she could think about was Drew and Elliot and the life that they were building together. As she envisioned the future, she could see Elliot's first steps, his first day of school, his first time driving a car, and his first day at college. And during each of those moments, she saw Drew standing by her side, smiling with her as they watched him grow.

But more than that, she was dreaming about the love and affection they might share one day.

Music would still be a part of the reality, but it no longer held the same power it had before. Something new was happening in her heart.

"Maybe," Drew said, taking a step closer to her as he moved aside a tendril of hair that had fallen across her face. "You can have every dream your heart desires."

Her breath paused as she stared into his eyes. What was he saying? Could he see the dream growing within her? Or was he speaking in generalities?

"I know Ed would love to have you sing tonight," Drew said, "and the crowd will be kind and forgiving, though I don't think they'll need to be. You'll be amazing."

She looked toward the pavilion. "There are so many people."

"Then sing just for me."

Whitney's heart began to pound hard as she considered what he was saying. Maybe she could do it, if she was focusing on Drew alone.

"I really want you to sing at the clubhouse on Tuesday," he said. "And if that means warming up here tonight, then I will do anything to get you up on that stage."

"Anything?"

He nodded.

"Did you register to play in the qualifying tournament on Tuesday?" She studied him. He had said he would, but he hadn't mentioned it again, so she wasn't sure.

Drew looked away for a second. "I registered—but, to be honest, I haven't decided if I'm really going to play."

"Just like I said I'd sing for your event, but I'm having doubts?" She couldn't fault him since she was struggling, too.

"But you have to sing," he said. "Not only because I want you to, but because

Professor Perkins agreed to come and listen to you. His connections alone can propel you on the path to fulfilling your dreams."

Sean Perkins was the music professor from the University of Minnesota, married to Drew's cousin. The one she'd embarrassed herself in front of last time. She longed to talk to him about his work—about what it would take for her to start her own school. Granted, she didn't need to sing in front of him for that opportunity, but would she have the courage and confidence to speak to him if he still saw her as the woman who couldn't even sing at a wedding? She needed to sing at the tournament to not only prove something to him—but to herself.

"Did you tell him who I was?" Whitney asked. "The one who messed up at the wedding?"

"He knows who you are, Whitney. And despite what you think, you didn't mess up as badly as you remember. I told him you studied at Berklee College of Music in Boston and want to start teaching. He messaged me back and said he was very interested in speaking to you and was excited to hear you sing. He'll be here on Tuesday."

The anxiety Whitney had felt at the idea of singing in front of a crowd now turned to panic. Getting a second chance was something she had never anticipated, but it only meant that the stakes were higher. If she messed up again, she'd be mortified to speak to him and it would make his trip to Timber Falls pointless.

"Maybe he shouldn't come," she said as she walked down the path a little way. "You should message him back and tell him it's not worth his time."

Drew followed her down the path and took her hand in his. "I'm not going to tell him to cancel his plans, Whitney. I know you want this more than you want anything else. And I'm not going to let you give in to fear this time. I know what fear can do to your dreams—I'm guilty of it myself. But we're going to do this together." He motioned toward the pavilion with his head. "You and me. No one else matters. If we fail, if we succeed, we do it together."

Affection flooded Whitney's heart. No one had ever offered to stand beside her, regardless of the outcome. There had always been conditions.

She wrapped her fingers through his, holding on to him as if he was a lifeline.

"You won't laugh at me or think less of me if I run off the stage in panic?"

Drew's eyes softened and he took a step closer to Whitney, so close she could feel the warmth off his body. "I could never laugh at you. I respect and admire you far too much."

She swallowed the rise of emotions and nodded. "If your friend is okay with me singing tonight, then I'll do it."

A grin spread across Drew's face, making him even more attractive than usual—

because his pleasure was directed at her. Suddenly, her knees were a little weaker and her stomach did somersaults, and not just because she'd agreed to sing in front of a crowd. If he only knew the power his smile and attention had on her, he would be stunned.

She'd do almost anything for him to smile at her like that again.

He was still holding her hand as he led her to the pavilion along the banks of the Mississippi River. Whether he realized it or not, she wasn't sure. But she was thankful for his strength and the anchor he provided by his presence.

It didn't take long for him to get his friend's attention and to make the introductions. Ed Carper was enthusiastic and excited for Whitney to sing with the orchestra. The musicians were ready for a break, and during that time, Ed set up a microphone and told everyone that Whitney would join them for a couple of songs during the second set.

"I have a list of our songs," Ed said as he brought out a three-ring binder. "Let us know which ones you can sing and we'll accommodate."

Whitney took the binder, glancing at Drew. He smiled, and she began perusing the list.

There were several songs she knew by heart and it wasn't hard for her to pick the one she wanted to sing. Ed insisted she sing more than one, so she tentatively chose a second.

By the time the orchestra was ready to go again, she was shaking so hard she had developed the cold sweats and felt like she might be sick.

But every time she looked at Drew and saw the eager anticipation on his face, or the complete faith in her ability shining from his eyes, she clung to it and it gave her courage.

She could do this—if not for her, then for Drew, who seemed to believe in her more than she had ever believed in herself.

* * *

The orchestra began to take their places again as Drew left the backstage of the pavilion and joined the others on the dance floor. He knew several people there and smiled at a few, though he didn't make a move to speak to them. Whitney was about to take the stage and he didn't want to miss a moment of her performance.

Ed came to the microphone as a soft breeze blew off the river. He wore a tuxedo, as did the other gentlemen in the chamber orchestra. The ladies were all in long, black gowns.

Everyone quieted as they turned their attention to the conductor.

"We have a very special guest this evening," Ed said with a grin on his face. "Whitney Keelan has agreed to sing a few songs for us."

Everyone on the dance floor clapped politely, though Drew saw a few confused faces. People might remember Whitney Emmerson from her high school days when she had sung in the choir and in the local musicals. But Whitney Keelan was a new name to them, a name that made his chest puff up with pride. He was honored that she had chosen to take his name.

Whitney stepped onto the stage. She had taken off her jean jacket and was still wearing her black dress and the red scarf. He would have never guessed that she had been a last-minute addition to the orchestra. She looked like she fit in perfectly with everyone else on stage.

He could see the nervousness behind her pretty smile, but when she found him in the audience, he nodded encouragement and it seemed to help her. Knowing that he could offer her strength bolstered his confidence.

It took a few seconds, but the orchestra lifted their instruments and Ed positioned his hands to begin.

Whitney stepped up to the microphone, visibly swallowing and taking a deep breath.

The orchestra began to play. For a second, Drew didn't recognize the tune, but then Whitney began to sing and he knew it immediately. It was "A Thousand Years" from Christina Perri.

She looked at Drew as she sang, and he felt as if it was just the two of them, after all.

Something stronger than pride or pleasure filled his chest. He was honored that she would look at him, that she would sing for him.

Instead of dancing, almost everyone else on the dance floor stared at Whitney. Her voice was so pure and so powerful, how could they not watch her? She was stunning and her voice was mesmerizing.

But the entire time, she only looked at Drew. The song spoke of loving someone for a thousand years, and then loving them for a thousand more.

In that moment, Drew wished she was saying those words for his ears alone—that she was speaking the truth from her heart and not singing lyrics to a song that someone else wrote.

Because he wanted it to be true. He wanted Whitney to love him. It wasn't enough to just be married. In less than two weeks, Drew had come to realize he wanted so much more than a marriage in name only. He wanted to be her husband in every sense of the word. He wanted to have her and to hold her, for better, for worse, for richer, for poorer, in sickness and in health, until death parted them. He knew it like he'd never known anything else before. The certainty of it overwhelmed him.

But was it something Whitney would want? She was grieving deeply, trying to deal with not only the loss of her family, but the pain of their separation and unresolved issues. Even if she leaned into him, would it be real? Would she know her own heart while it was so raw and broken?

Drew was falling in love with his wife, but he knew better than to push her for the things he wanted. She needed time to heal and he would give her that time, allow her to come to him without doubt or uncertainty—if she wanted to come to him at all.

Right now, it was enough that she was looking to him for strength and encouragement.

Maybe, with time and all the love he could offer her, she would choose to look to him for something more. Something deeper and of more infinite value.

Maybe she would love him in return.

Eventually, the others began to dance, though they kept their gazes fixed on Whitney.

Slowly, a smile began to lift the corners of her lips and she closed her eyes to sing the chorus of the song.

Drew watched her, breathless, as she was transformed. He hardly recognized her, and somehow, though he didn't think it was possible, she became even more beautiful to him.

Whatever fear or misgivings she'd had before appeared to have vanished and she owned the stage.

Ed glanced over his shoulder at her, and then at Drew, and winked before he turned back to his orchestra with a grin on his face.

Even the orchestra seemed to be playing better as they followed Whitney's leading. She was made for this moment, this stage, and this song. And he knew he wasn't the only person who felt it. The entire pavilion seemed to be lit up with her energy and glow.

She opened her eyes again and found Drew's gaze, smiling just for him, as if she was saying thank-you.

He wanted to reach up to put his hand over his thudding heart, but all he could do was watch and listen. How was it possible that he could have the depth of these feelings for her so soon? And how was it possible that she didn't know? Wasn't it obvious? Even now, couldn't she see it written all over his face?

When the song came to an end, the pavilion exploded with applause and Drew clapped the loudest of all.

Whitney's cheeks were pink and she was so graceful and elegant and humble as she motioned to the orchestra. Ed shook his head and gestured for her to take a bow.

She did, causing more applause.

Ed turned back to the musicians and lifted his hands again to start the next song. This one was "My Heart Will Go On."

If Drew thought she had sung the last one with heart and soul, it was nothing compared to this song. Again, the audience was enraptured.

Whitney should be pursuing her dream to teach and sing. Drew knew that with certainty. The only thing standing in her way was her fear. He would change that if he could.

When the song came to an end, and the audience had applauded once again, Whitney bowed and then left the stage, much to the dismay of the dancers and the musicians who begged her for another song.

Drew met her backstage, a smile on his face.

"You were incredible," he said, shaking his head as he put his hands on her arms. "I had no idea, Whitney. I mean, I knew you could sing, but what you just did, without any practice, was brilliant."

Her cheeks were flushed and her eyes were shining. "Thank you."

The orchestra began to play "To Make You Feel My Love," but without Whitney singing, it didn't have the power of the two previous songs.

She was still grinning. "Thank you for encouraging me. I haven't felt this alive in years. I actually did it, Drew. I sang my heart out and I didn't mess up and I didn't run off the stage in a panic."

"I knew you could do it."

Her face became serious as she looked at him. "I was able to do it only because of you."

"Me?" He frowned, lowering his hands from her arms.

"At the beginning, I felt panicky—but all I had to do was look at your face, see the confidence in your eyes, and I started to believe I could do it. And I did."

Without warning, she pressed against him and wrapped her arms around the back of his neck.

His surprise soon turned to pleasure and he embraced her.

"Thank you," she said again, this time quieter, her lips close to his ear.

They were already in each other's arms, so he began to move his feet to the sound of the song. His heart echoing the lyrics that were playing in his mind.

When the rain is blowing in your face, and the whole world is on your case, I would offer you a warm embrace to make you feel my love.

Chapter Eleven

Whitney knew her face was still glowing the next morning as she and Drew walked into Timber Falls Community Church with Elliot in his car seat. She knew, because she had looked at herself in the mirror while getting ready that morning and couldn't stop herself from grinning.

It felt marvelous to be on stage again, to be singing, sharing music like she was born to do. That stage had been hers and everyone there had known it—and for the first time since college, she had known and believed it, too.

If it hadn't been for Drew, she might never have had the courage to try again.

She glanced at him as he held the door open for her and met his quiet smile with one of her own.

Something had shifted last night, something she couldn't quite define, but it was there and it was palpable. Whether it was the way he looked at her, or the way she felt when she looked at him, or a combination of the two, she wasn't sure. But it had happened while she'd been on stage. He had offered her his strength and she had felt it, clung to it, and channeled it into her voice. No one had ever done that for her before, and she was certain no one else could.

But it was more than that. When she sang, it had been to Drew. The lyrics had come alive and had felt so real. They were no longer just words—they were truth echoing from her heart to his, communicating things that she wasn't yet ready to admit to herself.

And that communication was still echoing between them today. From the moment she'd gone into the kitchen to get her morning cup of coffee, to now as they entered the church, she felt a pull toward Drew, as if she never wanted to leave his side again. As if she could be completely content to be with him, and only him, for the rest of her life.

It was both thrilling and terrifying.

What if he wasn't feeling it? What if she was imagining it, because of the way she'd felt last night on stage?

"Good morning," Pastor Jacob said as he greeted Whitney and Drew with a smile. "It's nice to see you again."

The pastor's greeting pulled her out of her reverie.

She'd met Pastor Jacob last week, but they hadn't had much time to chat. He was tall, with a kind face and expressive eyes. From what Whitney had heard, he was a busy family man with a wife, a nine-year-old daughter, four-year-old triplet boys, and an eighteen-month-old daughter. His wife, Kate, had been at a retreat the previous weekend, so Whitney hadn't met her yet.

"Good morning," Whitney said.

"Kate," Pastor Jacob called to a pretty woman standing with a few people. "I'd like you to meet Drew's new wife."

Kate excused herself from the group she was talking to and turned toward her husband. She moved with confidence and grace, her face wreathed with a welcoming smile. "Hello."

"Hi." Whitney returned the smile.

"This is Whitney," Pastor Jacob said to his wife. "She and Drew were married a couple weeks ago."

"I heard," Kate said as she shook Whitney's hand. "Congratulations."

Whitney glanced at Drew, who was smiling at her. It still amazed her that Drew was her husband. This kind, handsome, intelligent man had chosen her—

in a way. And he seemed so pleased with that choice.

"Thank you," Whitney finally said.

"Where did you come from?" Kate asked. "I know you're Cricket's sister, but I didn't think you were living in town."

"I was in Washington, DC," Whitney said.

"Whitney attended Berklee College of Music in Boston," Drew told Kate and Jacob. "She hopes to open a school of music someday. She's an incredible singer."

"I was a singer—well, I suppose I still am." Kate chuckled. "If you count lullabies and birthday songs."

"You sing on the worship team," Jacob reminded her. "And for weddings once in a while."

Kate put her hand on her husband's arm and nodded. "You're right."

"What she means," Jacob said to Whitney, "is that she used to sing on Broadway."

Whitney's lips parted at the comment. "Really?"

"I was playing Fantine on the Broadway tour of *Les Misérables* before I came to Timber Falls," she said. "It was my dream job—until I met Jacob and realized God had a different plan for my life."

Jacob smiled at his wife as she looked up at him with tenderness.

Whitney looked at Drew again. He was watching her with that same expression he wore last night—the one filled with a depth of meaning she wasn't ready to unpack.

"Speaking of plan," Kate said, "I need to run to the nursery with our daughter's diaper bag before the worship service starts."

"I'll come with you," Whitney offered. "I'm hoping to leave Elliot in the nursery, too."

Whitney took the car seat as Drew said, "I'll find us a spot to sit in the sanctuary."

She nodded and followed Kate through

the entryway, down a hallway and into the nursery.

There were two older ladies in the nursery, ready to accept Elliot with open arms.

"Whitney," Kate said to her, "this is Mrs. Evans and Mrs. Topper."

"We met last week," Mrs. Evans said to Kate. "Piper and Max stood up for them at their wedding."

Mrs. Evans was Max's mom and one of the church ladies who served faithfully. Drew had warned her that there was a gaggle of ladies who liked to do more than just serve—they were known matchmakers and busybodies who meant well.

After leaving Elliot in their capable hands, she and Kate left the nursery.

The hallway was quiet as they walked back toward the sanctuary.

"You and Drew seem really happy together," Kate said to Whitney. "I know how hard it can be when life throws you a curve ball, but it's so much easier when you have a happy marriage to focus your energy into."

Whitney's footsteps faltered. "Drew and I aren't—I mean, we didn't—" She wasn't sure how to tell Kate the truth—or why she wanted to. "We married for Elliot's sake, not because we were in love."

Kate stopped, her face revealing her dismay. "I'm so sorry, Whitney. I didn't mean to presume. I should have kept my thoughts to myself—but the way you two looked at each other, I just assumed…"

"The way we looked at each other?" Were Whitney's thoughts and feelings so obvious? She'd been questioning herself since last night, and had thought she saw a shift in Drew—but did they look like they were in love?

More importantly, did it look like Drew was in love with her?

"You just look so happy and pleased with each other. I thought it was love, but perhaps it's just good friendship." Kate smiled. "I hope I haven't insulted you or—"

"Goodness, no." Whitney put her hand on Kate's arm to quiet her apology. "I was just surprised. I do care for Drew, very much." She paused and swallowed the emotions welling up within her. "He means more to me than I ever expected. But I don't think he loves me—at least, not romantically."

Kate's smile was slow and certain. "I've seen my fair share of love, and I think you might be surprised to learn your husband's feelings for you are deeper than you realize."

They continued down the hall, but Kate had to join the worship team, so she stopped near a side door. "If you'd ever like to join the worship team, we'd love to have you. We practice on Wednesday nights at seven."

"Thanks for the invitation. I'll think about it." Whitney smiled as Kate entered the back stage.

It would be nice to join the worship team and feel like she was offering something to the church—and to God. Just thinking about singing weekly gave her a sense of purpose, outside caring for Elliot.

She walked toward the sanctuary, Kate's words about Drew bouncing around in her mind and heart. Did Drew have deeper feelings for her? Her relationship with him was nothing like the one she'd had with Brock. It didn't feel all-consuming. It didn't feel like it would swallow her whole if she wasn't careful. And she'd thought she was in love with Brock.

Was love something different? Was she falling in love with Drew?

More importantly, was he falling in love with her? And if he was, how long would it be before he realized that loving her was a mistake? Something that almost everyone eventually regretted?

The thought of him looking at her the same way Brock had looked at her the day they broke up made her chest ache like nothing ever had.

Drew stood by the sanctuary doors, waiting for Whitney to join him. He'd made small talk with several people, while waiting for her to reappear.

But the worship band was coming onto the stage and people were starting to find their seats.

Where was she?

If he sat somewhere in the middle of the sanctuary, she would have a hard time finding him. The room was pretty large and he didn't want her to feel uncomfortable. But he also didn't like to stand by the doors and draw attention to himself while the worship band started to sing.

Eventually, he decided to sit near the back, close to the doors, where he could watch for her.

"Hello, Drew," said Mrs. Caruthers, one of the church ladies who had tried, in vain, to match him with a wife for years.

He smiled a greeting at her.

"I heard you finally tied the knot." Mrs. Caruthers beamed, as if she had done the tying herself. "But don't tell me that the rumors are true and you got married at the courthouse!"

Drew let out a breath. "It's true."

"For shame," Mrs. Caruthers said, shaking her head. "And you such a good boy, too."

He wasn't sure why she was scolding him, or why he wouldn't be a good boy if he got married at the courthouse. "We needed to get married as quick as we could."

"Every girl deserves a proper wedding, Drew. You should know that much. How are you going to rectify the situation? Will you at least have a reception so we can properly congratulate the two of you? Maybe at that fancy clubhouse of yours?"

A proper reception? The thought hadn't even occurred to Drew. "I don't think—"

"You know what we'll do." Mrs. Caruthers moved closer to him on the pew as the first worship song began to play. "We'll hold a bridal shower for your bride—it's the least we can do until that wedding reception."

"You've all been so nice, bringing meals the past couple of weeks. We don't need anything more—really."

"Nonsense."

Kate called the congregation to stand, so Drew did—with Mrs. Caruthers at his side—and looked toward the door for a sign of Whitney.

Where was she? Had something happened to Elliot? Was something wrong with her?

"We'll plan the bridal shower and surprise Whitney—won't that be nice?" Mrs. Caruthers nodded, as if answering her own question. "Don't breathe a word of it to her, Drew. The ladies and I will take care of all the details."

She moved back to her husband's side, a satisfied smile on her face.

And still, Whitney did not come.

They were in the middle of the third worship song when he decided to go and check on her.

He left the sanctuary and walked toward the hall leading to the nursery—and that was where he found Whitney, standing outside the pastor's office, looking at some pictures on the wall.

Pictures of the couples from church who had either been married in the building or by the pastor. It had been a tradition for a newly married couple to provide an eight-by-ten portrait of their wedding day to the church. There were dozens and dozens of happy couples, some in black-and-white from the early part of the century, all the way through to the present. It was fun to look at the pictures and see how styles had changed. The most recent pictures were of couples similar in age to Whitney and Drew. Max and Piper were up there, along with Nate and Adley—and even Pastor Jacob and Kate.

But there was no picture of Drew and Whitney—and there wouldn't be, since they hadn't been married at the church or by the pastor. And come to think of it, no one had taken a picture that day.

"Is everything okay?" Drew asked Whitney, speaking quietly so he wouldn't startle her.

She turned at the sound of his voice, and though she didn't look surprised to see him, she still looked startled.

Concern wound its way around his heart. He put his hand on her arm. "Are you okay, Whitney?"

She looked back at the pictures, paying attention to Jacob and Kate's portrait. "They all look so happy, don't they?"

Did she regret not having a wedding? Was Mrs. Caruthers right? Of course she was right. Whitney *did* deserve a wedding. But was it right to have one if they weren't truly married?

"They do look happy," he said, coming to stand closer to her. He longed to draw her into his arms like last night. She smelled sweet, like a bouquet of flowers. But he didn't have the right. "Are you upset we didn't have a real wedding?"

"No." She shook her head, but her face didn't match her word.

"If you want a real wedding, we can. I'd—"

"Why would we have a real wedding when we don't have a real marriage?"

Her words cut through him—not because they were mean or hurtful, but because they were true. He wanted to tell her he longed for a real marriage, but he didn't know if she was ready, and he'd promised himself he wouldn't push her.

Yet—he also wanted to be clear that he was willing. "I'll do whatever you wish," he said. "If you want a real wedding—or a real marriage..." He let the words trail off.

Whitney turned and looked at him, blinking several times, as if she wasn't sure she heard him correctly.

It was quiet in the hall, though the notes

from the worship music were echoing throughout the building.

Neither one spoke for a bit, but then Whitney took a step away from him. "We should get into the sanctuary. I'd hate to miss the service."

Just like that, the moment was over. Whether or not Whitney understood his meaning, he couldn't be certain. If she had, then she had turned away, rejecting his offer. If she hadn't, then he wasn't sure if he should reiterate.

No. They'd just return to how they'd been. Pretend like he hadn't said anything.

It would be easier that way.

At least, that was what he'd have to tell his heart.

Chapter Twelve

Drew's comment was still twirling around in Whitney's head on Monday afternoon as she walked through the grocery store. He'd said it so gently and with such tenderness that she'd thought she misheard him. "I'll do whatever you wish," he'd said. "If you want a real wedding—or a real marriage..."

She had been looking at the wedding pictures on the wall and had turned to see if she'd heard him correctly. But as she studied his face and thought about all they'd been through, she was almost certain he hadn't meant it.

Yet, what if he had been offering a marriage, in the real sense of the word? Did that mean he was falling in love with her? He hadn't said he loved her. Sometimes, she thought she glimpsed it in the way he looked at her, or in the words he spoke, but he was just as kind and gentle with Elliot. Perhaps it was just his way.

But they had only been together for two weeks. How could he be in love with her in two weeks?

Around and around the questions turned in her mind.

Elliot was in his car seat in the basket of the shopping cart. He had been sleeping for a couple of hours, allowing Whitney to run errands. She just needed a few things from the grocery store and then they could get home.

The produce section of the store was bursting with color. Red, green, purple, orange and yellow fruits and vegetables called out to be noticed. Whitney had decided to make a simple meal of BLT sandwiches and French fries for supper. Drew had left early that morning, well before the sun had come up, and he had texted her a few hours later, telling her not to worry about his supper. With the big tournament the next day, he wasn't sure what time he would get home.

So Whitney picked up a small head of lettuce and a ripe tomato, her mind still on Drew and whether or not he had really offered a marriage the day before.

Elliot started to wiggle in his car seat. Whitney stopped pushing the cart and leaned down to put his pacifier back into his mouth. He sucked on it a few times and then spat it out, starting to fuss again.

Whitney still had several things on her shopping list to pick up, and it was hard to get out of the house with a baby in tow, so she didn't want to leave without finishing. She tried the pacifier again, but he didn't want it.

Thankfully, she had water in a bottle, so she quickly mixed in some formula and took him out of his car seat, there in the produce section, to try to feed him. It wasn't ideal, but it would have to do. She could feed him and still shop—maybe.

After she had him in the crook of her arm, she tried to give him his bottle. He sucked for a few seconds and then screwed up his face and cried hard. Whitney tapped the nipple of the bottle against his lips and he sucked again, but then cried.

Whitney set the bottle in the cup holder on the shopping cart and brought Elliot up to her shoulder to try and burp him. She bounced him as she met the gaze of several people who were shopping. A couple of ladies gave her an empathetic look— but one older lady was clearly not happy with the noise. She gave Whitney a scathing glance and then pushed her cart out of the produce section, shaking her head, mumbling something about keeping kids at home where they belonged.

Elliot continued to cry, his little wails so heart-wrenching, that Whitney was worried he was in real pain. She tried again to feed him, but he didn't seem to want the bottle. Nothing she did was working. He didn't need to be changed, so what was wrong?

From around the corner, another woman walked into the produce section—someone Whitney would rather not see at the moment.

"What's wrong with him?" Paula asked as she pushed her cart toward Whitney, concern on her face. "He sounds like you're pinching him."

"I'm not pinching him," Whitney said with a tight mouth, though she wasn't sure Paula heard her over Elliot's crying.

"Is he hungry?"

Whitney didn't want to deal with Paula, especially now. But she also didn't want to leave her half-full shopping cart in the produce section and have to come back and finish later.

"I tried to feed him," Whitney said over his wails. "He won't eat."

"Let me try." Paula reached for Elliot without being invited.

Whitney could have pulled him back, but there were eyes on them and she didn't want to make a scene.

"Shh, honey," Paula said as she bounced Elliot and secured him in her arms, slipping one of his arms under hers and holding him more like he was nursing. She grabbed the bottle and placed it into his mouth.

Elliot latched onto the bottle as if he was dying of hunger and began sucking on it with vengeance. His tears stopped and he looked up at Paula, staring at her face as he drank his bottle.

"There," Paula said in a syrupy-sweet voice. "You just needed someone who knows what they're doing. He was nursed by Cricket for the first few weeks of his life and he still needs to believe he's being fed that way. It makes him feel more secure and loved."

Whitney pressed her lips together, breathing hard out of her nose. "I know what I'm doing, Paula. I've been feeding him for almost two weeks."

"*Do* you know what you're doing?" Paula didn't take her eyes off Elliot. "It didn't sound like you did."

It took all of Whitney's willpower to keep her peace and not lash out at Paula. All that mattered now was that Elliot was eating and no longer crying. When he was done, Whitney could finish her shopping and go home where she'd have a little peace again.

They stood there for a few minutes as Elliot ate and Paula finally said, "Elliot and I had a visitor the other day when he was over at my house."

"Oh?" Whitney didn't really care who had been to visit them.

"Heather Sinclair stopped by when I told her Elliot was at my house." Paula swayed slightly as she continued to look at Elliot. "We had such a good time. She's amazing with Elliot—and he absolutely adored her. I'm not surprised, since she's such a natural with him."

At the sound of Heather's name, Whitney lifted her chin. It was hard enough that Drew worked with her and she had to wonder about the nature of their relationship. Now Whitney had to compete with Heather for Elliot's affection, too?

"You do realize that Heather and Drew were an item before you came." Paula finally looked up at Whitney.

Whitney crossed her arms, wishing she could take back Elliot and be done with Paula, but she was too afraid he'd start to cry again.

"He would have married her, too, if you hadn't come along." Paula's lips pursed as she shook her head. "Heather would have made such a good mom to Elliot, and I think Drew is going to realize really soon what a mistake he made by not marrying her."

Paula's words made Whitney freeze inside. The same sense of panic that she felt while she was singing for a crowd began to seize upon her. Paula was right—it was only a matter of time before Drew realized the truth. Everyone else could see it—why couldn't he?

"I can see that you know I'm right." Paula lifted Elliot to her lips and kissed his tiny head. "The only question is, what will you do about it?"

Whitney bit her bottom lip, shaking her head as tears stung the backs of her eyes. She didn't want to cry in front of Paula. "Why haven't you ever liked me? From the time we were kids until now you have tried to make my life miserable." Whitney swiped at one of the tears that slipped out of her eye, angry that she couldn't stop it from falling. "Why?"

Paula lifted her gaze and stared hard at Whitney. "I never tried to make your life miserable. I simply tried to get you to understand what everyone else could see, but you couldn't. You've never fit in with us. Period. I've tried helping you see the truth so you'd stop embarrassing your-self." She lifted a shoulder. "You didn't fit with Cricket and me—and you don't fit with Drew and Elliot. The sooner you stop trying, the easier it will be on you."

Whitney's lips trembled with anger and pain. She reached for Elliot, causing his bottle to slip out of his mouth and hit the floor. He instantly began to cry, but Whitney needed to get out of the grocery store. She set him back into his car seat and fumbled with the latches.

Her tears were threatening to come with full force, so she simply stopped messing with the straps and pushed the cart out of the produce section. She hurried down the main aisle and left all of her groceries near one of the checkout counters as she took Elliot out and left the building.

She tried keeping her emotions in check, but it was difficult. Paula's words were painful, because they were true. She'd al-ways known it, but had started to believe that maybe she'd finally found a place to fit in, with Drew and Elliot.

It was clear she had been deceiving herself and everyone knew it, except her.

She was able to get Elliot properly latched into his car seat as she tried to soothe him with her voice. He was still crying, his little chin quivering as tear drops formed in his eyes.

Whitney got into her car and pulled out of the parking lot.

The house was about a ten-minute drive from the store. She tried hard to keep her tears at bay as she drove. Eventually, Elliot began to quiet and Whitney hoped he had fallen asleep.

When she finally pulled into the driveway at Cricket's house, she put the car in Park and turned off the engine.

Sunlight sparkled on the river as she stared straight ahead, Paula's words clenching her heart and making her relive each moment with Drew these past two weeks. Had she ever fit into his world? She had thought so—had hoped—but maybe she wasn't able to see clearly. Maybe she had blinders on her eyes and heart and she was only seeing what she wanted to see.

Because she desperately wanted a home, a family, a place to belong. And Drew was the first person to offer it to her.

She put her forehead on the steering wheel and allowed the tears to finally come.

Whitney wept. All the pain from the past four years—and longer still—seemed to pour out of her heart as she cried. Her grief was deep and she didn't try to hold it back.

The worst of her tears came when she thought about Drew and the hope she'd started carrying for their future. Two weeks wasn't long enough to know if a relationship had what it would take for a lifetime, and she'd been misleading herself to think otherwise. Drew and Heather had years of knowing each other—and Paula was right. Heather was the obviously better choice for Drew. She had a place in his world, had a history with him, and knew how to take care of Elliot, just like Paula did. Whitney hadn't been able to get him to quiet down and Paula had swooped in and managed it without trouble.

If Whitney couldn't handle one little episode in the produce section, how was she going to handle things when they got really difficult?

And what would she do about tomorrow? She had hired a babysitter from the church and was planning to be at the tournament to cheer on Drew—but now she wasn't so sure she wanted to be there. Drew would inevitably introduce her as his wife. What would his colleagues and others think when they saw whom he had married—worse, with her frame of mind, what might happen when she got up and sang for them? She couldn't embarrass him that way.

She *wouldn't* embarrass him that way.

* * *

"What do you think?" Heather asked Drew as they stood outside the clubhouse, inspecting the fleet of golf carts that sat parked in a row, washed and ready to be put into service tomorrow.

"Everything looks great," Drew said as he put his clipboard under his arm, admiring the freshly manicured greens, the recently resurfaced parking lot and the sparkling windows on the clubhouse. "I can't believe we got everything checked off our to-do list so early."

"Maybe you should take the evening off and rest up." Heather smiled at Drew. "You've got a big day tomorrow. Your first competition in years."

"I have a tee time at four for one last practice with a few of the PGA officials who are coming in this afternoon. I'll make sure everything's been taken care of on the course."

"I personally drove the course earlier today to check." Heather put her hand on

Drew's arm. "It's perfect. I don't think we could do one more thing to be ready."

Drew took a deep breath and nodded.

"All you need to worry about is playing the best round of your life tomorrow." Heather squeezed his arm. "I'll take care of the rest."

He smiled and shook his head. "What will I do without you after you leave? You haven't changed your mind?"

Heather dropped her hand from his arm and turned toward one of the pots of plants near the front door. She picked a few deadheads from the geraniums and lifted a shoulder. "You know I can't stay, Drew."

"I don't get it." He shrugged, trying not to be frustrated.

"I know you don't, and that's part of the problem." A group of golfers came off the eighteenth hole and entered the clubhouse.

Other than nodding a greeting at them, neither one spoke until the golfers were in the building.

Heather turned to face Drew, lifting her chin just a hair. "You never did realize how much I loved you—did you?"

Drew's mouth parted as he stared at her. "No." A sad smile tilted her lips. "I can see you didn't."

"Heather—"

"There's nothing left to say, Drew. Even if you had known, I don't think it would have mattered. You never loved me and would have married Whitney anyway." She studied him for a heartbeat. "Do you love her?"

Drew had hardly acknowledged his feelings to himself, let alone anyone else. And the first person who would know wouldn't be Heather. It would be Whitney.

"I'm sorry I hurt you." Drew wished things had been different. He wished Heather hadn't had feelings for him and they could keep working together. But if she *had* been in love with him—then it was best that she leave.

"That's why I love you, Drew. You *are*

sorry." She let out a sigh. "You didn't hurt me on purpose. If you had, it would be easier to get over you and to turn my love for you into anger and resentment. But—" she lifted a shoulder again "—I can't hate you, Drew."

"I wouldn't want you to."

Her smile was sad again as she said, "Does Whitney even know what she has in you? Does she deserve you?"

Drew didn't know if Whitney loved him, but he did know the answer to the second part of Heather's question. "If there's anyone in our relationship who isn't deserving, it's me. I've never met anyone like Whitney and I can't believe I'm the man who gets to be her husband."

Heather looked down at the ground for a second as she bit the inside of her mouth. When she finally looked up at him, she said, "You answered my first question. I can see how much you love her, just in the way your face lights up when you talk about her."

Drew wouldn't deny it—because he couldn't.

"I'll finish out the week," Heather said, "but Friday will be my last day."

"Thanks for all your hard work, Heather. I couldn't have gotten through the past few weeks without you."

"I know." She lifted her face and smiled. "I'm irreplaceable. And that's the only thing that makes me happy about leaving."

Drew laughed. When he finally quieted, he said, "Maybe I will head home to clean up a bit before my tee time. I've been here since five this morning." He looked at his watch. "I have about forty-five minutes before the officials will be here. Just enough time for a quick shower."

"I'll see you in the morning." Heather turned and entered the clubhouse.

He stood there for a second, trying to figure out how he would replace Heather, but decided he would worry about that after tomorrow. There was enough on his mind already.

A few minutes later, he was on his golf cart, heading toward home. Whitney would be surprised to see him, but he didn't think she'd mind. He didn't have much time to clean up before he needed to be back at the clubhouse to meet the officials, but he wanted to see Whitney and Elliot. He knew, without a doubt in his mind, that he would be able to play better if he could just see them for a few minutes. They refreshed and energized him better than anything else.

Drew pulled into the driveway, surprised to see Whitney's car parked outside. Ever since the furniture had been brought into the house, they had both been parking in the garage.

He parked the cart and started toward the house, but then he noticed Whitney was still in the vehicle. Her forehead was on the steering wheel—and for a split second, Drew's heart stopped. Was she hurt?

Without a second thought, he ran to her car and pulled the door open.

She looked up, her eyes going round. Tears streamed down her face and her nose was red.

They stared at each other until Drew said, "Whitney, what's wrong?"

She swallowed and wiped at her cheeks. "Nothing."

He frowned as he squatted down by the side of the car and put his hand on her arm. "No. It's not nothing. Is it Elliot? Is he okay?"

"He's fine." She grabbed a napkin from the center console and wiped at her face. "He's asleep in the back."

Drew glanced back there and saw that the baby was okay.

"What's wrong?" He asked again. "Something happened."

She took a shuddering breath and then moved to get out of the car. "Really. I'm fine. I just got overwhelmed and needed to let out some tears."

"Why are you overwhelmed? Do you need more help?"

"No." She shook her head and pushed her blond hair off her cheek. "Elliot got upset at the grocery store and I couldn't calm him. Paula—" She stopped talking.

"Paula? What did Paula do?"

Whitney refused to look at Drew as she spoke. "She was there and she got him to calm down when I couldn't."

Drew waited to hear the rest of the story, because he knew there had to be more. He'd never seen Whitney this upset. "What else happened, Whitney?"

She moved away from the car and closed the door, then she went to the back. "It's not a big deal. I don't want to bother you before the big tournament tomorrow. We can talk later."

He finally put his hand on her shoulder and forced her to look at him. He felt so helpless as he stared into her sad, brown eyes. "Tell me what's wrong, Whitney."

She stared at him for a couple of seconds and then crumpled into his chest.

He held her tight, wrapping her in a hug, wishing he could take away her pain.

"We shouldn't have gotten married, Drew," she said between sobs. "It was a mistake—and I knew it all along. I wanted to believe it would work, but—"

"Whitney, what are you talking about?" His heart was pounding hard at her words. He pulled away just enough to look into her eyes. "It wasn't a mistake."

"You haven't realized it yet, but you will—and when you do…" She trailed off.

"When I do, what?"

She shook her head and continued to cry. "It doesn't matter. *I* know it was a mistake."

His breath stilled. "You truly think getting married was a mistake?"

Whitney nodded as she pulled out of his arms, wiping at her face again. "It was too soon. We were both in shock. We didn't know what we were doing. We were scared."

Drew stared at her. "I knew exactly what I was doing."

She didn't seem to hear him as she turned toward the car. "I think we need to give this arrangement some serious thought, before anyone gets hurt."

Pain sliced through Drew's chest. Hurt? He was already hurting.

She faced away from him for a long time as neither one said a word. Finally, she let out a long breath and then turned back to look at him. "I didn't mean to spring this on you today, before the tournament. I was just—" She paused, as if at a loss for words. "I'm sorry. I thought I could dry my tears before you came home. I shouldn't have said anything until after tomorrow."

He stared at her, confusion clouding his thoughts. "I don't know what to say, Whitney. I thought things were going really well."

She crossed her arms and shook her head, but didn't say anything.

"I want to talk," he said as he looked at his watch, wishing he didn't have to meet the officials at four. "But I need to get back to the course. Tomorrow's a big day—for both of us." He was trying to find something solid to stand on—a bit of hope he could cling to as he tried to understand what was happening—and to get through the next twenty-four hours. "Can we just pause this conversation and talk more about it after the tournament?"

"Yeah." She nodded as she sniffled. "I'm sorry, Drew. Really, I am. I didn't expect you to find me this way."

"I know." He drew her into his arms again and held her tight. Something had happened—and he had a feeling Paula had been at the heart of it.

"I need to take a quick shower and get back to meet the PGA officials. They'll be at the course at four. I'm sorry we can't talk—"

"Go," she said as she wiped her face

with the napkin again. "I don't want to keep you. I'm sorry you saw me like this"

He touched her cheek, wishing he knew if it was wise to tell her how he felt, but sensing that it would only make matters worse right now. They needed time and space to work through their relationship.

"After the tournament," he said quietly.

She nodded. "After the tournament."

He tried to smile for her, but couldn't muster the strength, because he felt like his heart was breaking.

Chapter Thirteen

Whitney wasn't sure who she was more nervous for: herself or Drew. Tuesday morning had dawned bright and blue, with not a single cloud in the sky. The golf course was buzzing with the hundreds of people who had come for the big tournament. Most were spectators, but there were several players, some media and the golf course staff.

In the middle of all of it was Drew. Whitney hadn't seen him last night, since he'd come in late and she had purposely gone to bed early, not wanting to bother him before his big day. She was still angry with herself that he had seen her upset yesterday. The last thing she wanted to do was concern him with such an important issue, but she had not anticipated him coming home.

She still couldn't forget the look on his face when she had told him their marriage was a mistake—in that moment, she knew that he had fallen in love with her. At least, he thought he was in love with her. But it made it even worse. Knowing that he had feelings for her, and that it would be harder to convince him that their marriage *had* been a mistake, was plaguing her today.

The look in his eyes had told her that he wanted to fight for her—but where would that get them? Drew believed their marriage was a good idea, but everything Whitney had ever known about herself suggested otherwise. Paula's accusations still rang in her ears, as did her parents' lifelong disappointments. Whitney had never fit into the world that Drew occupied, and until she had married him, she thought she was okay with that reality. Someone like Heather fit his lifestyle better. And what Paula said was true: if Whitney hadn't shown up, Drew would have probably asked Heather to marry him instead.

Whitney knew she needed to leave, for both Drew and Elliot's sake. She wanted Drew to keep Elliot, so she would go to the judge and convince him to give Drew time to marry someone else—probably Heather. It was obvious that Heather loved Drew and she'd be better for Elliot, too.

Whitney's gaze landed on Heather. She was standing near the first tee, talking with a reporter. Her dark hair was pulled back into a ponytail and she was wearing a white sun visor, a white athletic skirt and a white long-sleeve pullover with a pink polo shirt underneath. She looked like the quintessential golfer, her skin tan, her smile big and bright, and her knowledge of the course second only to Drew's.

Drew was on the other side of the first tee box, speaking to a small group of men who looked like officials. They each held a walkie-talkie and wore a badge. As Drew spoke to them, Whitney admired his athletic form, his clean-cut looks and his confidence. Even if she hadn't known who he was, she would have guessed him to be one of the most important people at this tournament. He looked so sure of himself, so in control.

Her heart stirred as she watched him, realizing that her love for him ran deeper than she had first suspected. It felt like an achingly sweet pull in the center of her stomach, making her happier and sadder than she'd ever felt before. One look from him was all she wanted—a simple glance, an acknowledgement or even a smile— and she would feel like she was as light as air all day long.

Yet, she knew she shouldn't harbor such thoughts or feelings. Not today—not when she was planning how she would tell him she wanted an annulment.

"Whitney!" Piper Evans walked up to Whitney with a grin on her face. "I'm so happy I found you. I've been looking all over the place. It's so busy I didn't think I'd ever spot you."

"Hi, Piper." Whitney accepted the hug that her friend offered and she plastered a smile on her face so Piper wouldn't suspect what Whitney had been thinking about.

"Did you leave Elliot with a sitter?" Piper asked.

She nodded. "Mrs. Topper agreed to babysit him. She loved on him so well at church the other day. She told me that she misses having babies around and if I ever needed a sitter, she'd be willing. So I took her up on it."

"It's nice to have grandma-like figures in our children's lives." Piper's smile faltered a little. "My mom died when I was young, but we have Max's mom for our little Lainey—and the other church ladies who all love on her like she's their own."

"Your mom died?" Whitney frowned. "I'm sorry to hear that."

Piper nodded, her eyes filled with a sadness Whitney understood all too well. "When I was little, before we moved to Timber Falls. I only have a few memories of her."

Whitney turned her focus off herself and onto her friend. "You've had a lot of loss in your life, haven't you?"

"More than I like to think about sometimes. But you know what? God has been faithful the entire time and He's used each experience to draw me closer to Him—and to those who are still in my life."

Whitney glanced at Drew—and at that moment, he looked her way. It was the first time they'd had eye contact since yesterday in the driveway.

His face brightened at seeing her and he smiled.

Whitney held her breath, warmth filling her from head to toe. She returned the smile, wanting him to know how proud she was to be there and to see him pursue his dreams.

One of the officials said something to him and he turned away from Whitney—and the moment was over.

Piper didn't say anything, but she smiled and glanced away, a knowing look on her face.

"Max is volunteering today," Piper said. "Do you mind if I hang out with you while we watch the tournament? I think Joy Asher and Merritt Taylor will be here, too."

"I'd love some company." Whitney had met Joy and Merritt at church and was looking forward to getting to know them better, too.

The first tee time was drawing close, so an announcer stepped up to the microphone and asked everyone to quiet down.

"Welcome to the last of this year's PGA

US Open qualifying tournaments," he said into the microphone.

There was wild applause as several hundred people turned to look at the speaker.

"We are honored to be at the Timber Falls Golf Course owned and managed by Andrew Keelan." He turned and shook hands with Drew while everyone applauded. "Mr. Keelan would like to say something before we start."

Drew came up to the microphone and smiled at the crowd, searching until he found Whitney. Their gazes locked as he began to speak.

"Today is an exciting day for the staff here at Timber Falls Country Club. It's been a lifelong dream for us to welcome the PGA to host an event here, one that my late father and brother shared with me. I would like to dedicate today's tournament to their memory. To Bill and Sam Keelan. Thank you."

A quiet hush fell over the crowd, which

was then followed by a more sedate applause.

Whitney smiled at Drew, wishing his dad and brother were there to celebrate this huge accomplishment with him.

As Drew stepped back, Heather came forward and gave him a hug. She held him for a long time, and when she pulled back, she wiped her hand across her cheek. Drew said something to her and she nodded, then he hugged her again.

Whitney looked down at the program in her hands, trying to convince herself that she had been right all along and Drew belonged with Heather. It was better that way. They had a history together.

"Thank you, Mr. Keelan," the announcer said into the microphone. "Now, on to the rules. The top three players with the lowest scores at the end of eighteen holes will qualify to play in this year's PGA US Open."

Another chorus of cheers erupted. Whitney looked up again and wished that she hadn't.

Heather was now standing beside Drew and she smiled up at him as he glanced down at her and grinned.

Whitney couldn't watch anymore. She busied herself with looking over the program to read the names of all the golfers competing today.

"Each of the fifty-three golfers has been apprised of the rules and has been given their own scorecards," the announcer said. "There will be officials at each hole to watch the game, as well as volunteers who will keep each fairway free from spectators. Please honor the boundary lines and respect both the players and the other spectators." He smiled. "Now, let's play some golf!"

The crowd cheered again.

"This is so exciting," Piper said to Whitney as the first group of golfers walked up to the first tee box. "I have been praying for Drew the past few days. I hope he is in the top three winners today."

Whitney smiled, though she didn't feel like smiling, and nodded. "Me, too."

"And then tonight." Piper's voice was almost giddy. "I can't wait for the dance. Drew told Max you'll be singing. It's been a long time since I've had a day away from Lainey, and I can't remember the last time Max and I were at a dance together. It was probably Nate and Adley's wedding."

Whitney wished she felt as excited as Piper, but the truth was, she was terrified to sing tonight. She hadn't spotted Professor Perkins yet, but she knew he was still planning to come.

Maybe, if he liked what he heard tonight and he knew of a position open at the University of Minnesota, it would be just the thing Whitney needed to move forward. It would never, ever compare to Drew and Elliot, but it would be best for all of them. And it was something to focus on—a dream to cling to when all else felt like it was falling apart.

Drew could hardly believe they had finally arrived at the tournament. Years of applications, planning, hopes and dreams had come to fruition and his dad and Sam weren't even there to see it happen. It was bittersweet, but Drew was determined to enjoy it as much as he could, if for no other reason than to honor his father and brother.

It was late in the day and Drew had already played his round of golf. He'd gone out midmorning with a group of three other men. They'd finished an hour ago, but Drew had been so busy since he'd walked off the eighteenth green that he'd hardly looked at the leaderboard to see where he stood.

"The last foursome just teed off on the eighteenth hole," Heather said as she came up to Drew in the clubhouse lobby where he'd been answering questions from his head groundskeeper about a sprinkler system leak on the ninth hole. It was the worst time for it to happen, but the groundskeeper had assured him it was being taken care of.

"Wow," Drew said as he looked at his watch. "Where did the day go?"

Heather smiled. "It's been eventful. I can't believe it's almost over."

"Not quite. We still have the evening festivities."

"I almost forgot." Heather's voice was devoid of enthusiasm. "I haven't even seen Whitney today. Is she here? Shouldn't she be setting up or something?"

"She's here." At least, he hoped she was still there. He had caught a glimpse of her from time to time as he played his round of golf. She, Piper and a couple other ladies from church had followed him from hole to hole, but after congratulating him at the end of his round, they had walked off to watch the other golfers finish out their rounds.

That was the last he saw Whitney, though he hadn't stopped thinking about her, even with everything that was going on. Their conversation from yesterday had plagued his every move. He had lain awake far too late the night before, mulling over what she had said, trying to figure out what had happened to make her say it was all a mistake. Was it just because Paula had quieted Elliot when Whitney couldn't, or was it something more?

Each time he saw her today, he knew she was still thinking about it, just in the way she looked at him. Her smile was filled with a deep sadness, one that broke his heart.

He didn't want the tournament to end, but he couldn't wait to talk to Whitney and tell her she was wrong. Their marriage wasn't a mistake, and if she thought he didn't love her, he wanted to put her heart and mind at ease. Even if she wasn't ready to return his feelings, he wanted her to know that he'd be waiting for her.

A familiar man walked through the front door of the clubhouse just then, a smile on his aging face. "Hello, Drew."

Drew smiled a greeting at his cousin's husband. He'd been a professor at the University of Minnesota for as long as Drew had known him and was fascinating to talk to. "Welcome back to Timber Falls, Sean."

Heather nodded at Drew and then took her leave as Drew turned to shake Sean's hand.

"I heard you played a great round today," Sean said. "I saw your name on the leaderboard before I came inside to find you. You're in third place."

"I am?"

"The first three go to the US Open, don't they?" Sean asked.

Drew nodded, a little stunned. "There are two other groups out there, finishing up. I don't know if I'll hold on to third place."

"Well," Sean smiled, his white eyebrows

lifting with pleasure, "enjoy it while it's yours, whether you hold on to it or not. Right now, you're third." Sean was a tall man, thin and regal in bearing. He was wearing a blazer with elbow patches—the quintessential professor. "I'm sorry about Sam and Cricket." Sean shook his head, his face sobering. "What a horrible tragedy."

"Thanks." Drew nodded, still not comfortable accepting people's condolences. He didn't know how to respond, but appreciated their attempt.

"Where is Cricket's sister?" Sean asked, looking around. "Or should I say, your wife? Annabeth told me you two had married."

Annabeth was Drew's older cousin and Sean's wife.

"We did," Drew said, hoping and praying that Whitney would want to stay married after what she'd said last night.

"I'm eager to speak to her. I remember her well. If she could get past her nerves, I believe she's a talented singer." He looked around the lobby. "Is she here?"

"I think she's still out on the course, watching the final groups finish up. She'll be singing later this evening after supper." Drew couldn't help but feel proud of Whitney. "I think you're going to be really pleased that you agreed to come. I've never heard anyone else like her. She's extremely talented and well trained. I know she'll make an incredible teacher."

"I don't doubt it. Nerves are something that can be overcome, but natural talent isn't something that can be taught. I hope she won't let her nerves get the better of her tonight."

Drew planned to be there, close to the stage, to offer his strength and support if she needed it.

"Why don't you grab a cool drink on the house," Drew said to Sean. "I'm going to watch the last group finish up on the eighteenth hole."

"Thank you, I think I will get some iced tea." Sean left to find the beverage.

Drew walked out of the clubhouse and toward the back of the building where a large crowd of spectators had formed. The first person he noticed was Heather, who was standing at the back of the crowd. She noticed him, too, and motioned him over.

"One of the players is a stroke behind you," Heather said quietly. "If he birdies this hole, you'll be tied and you'll need to face off with him to see who goes to the US Open."

Drew looked up at the leaderboard and saw his name in third place with the other guy's name right below his. His heart started to pound as he looked out toward the fairway where the last of the golfers were just cresting the rise. He had no idea how many strokes his competition had taken yet, but he could sense the tension in the air and knew that it was close.

"If he pars this hole," Heather said, close

to Drew, her eyes lit up with excitement, "you're going to the US Open!"

Drew couldn't believe he was this close to realizing his dream—and all he could think about right now was Whitney. He scanned the crowd, trying to find her. There were hundreds of people standing around the eighteenth green and it felt almost impossible to differentiate one person from the other.

But then, he saw her. She was wearing a long sundress. Her blond hair was flowing down her back and she was smiling at the women standing near her.

His breath caught at seeing her and he wondered if he would always have that reaction, because he would never tire of it. She was so beautiful to him—and not just on the outside. He loved her with all of his heart, and he couldn't think of anyone else he wanted by his side if he went to the US Open.

She was so far away that he would never be able to get to her side by the time the golfers were finished with this hole, so he stood where he was, admiring her from afar, trying to keep his focus on her and not his nerves.

Her gaze went to the leaderboard and then she scanned the crowd and finally saw him.

The smile she offered him made his knees weak. She pointed at the board and grinned.

He nodded, wishing she was at his side, sharing this moment with him.

Her gaze shifted and her smile disappeared. When he looked to see what she was staring at, he saw Heather. Just a foot away from him.

When he glanced back at Whitney, she was no longer looking in his direction, but had shifted her gaze back to the players on the course.

Disappointment sliced through Drew as the players each took a turn chipping onto the green. The crowd clapped and Drew held his breath. He didn't know who the man was on the leaderboard under his name, so he'd have to wait until the crowd told him who had won.

It was agonizing to wait. Drew had never felt like a game took as long as the last few minutes of that hole.

And when the last golfer tapped his ball toward the hole—and it missed—there was a great sigh of disappointment from the crowd, and then people started to turn to Drew.

"Congratulations," an older woman said to him, taking his hand into hers. "You did it! You're going to the US Open!"

Drew's mouth slipped open as more and more people started to congratulate him.

Heather threw her arms around his neck and gave him a big hug. "I knew you could do it!"

He felt like he was in a daze as he hugged her back and then started shaking the hands of dozens of others.

The entire time, he searched the crowd

for Whitney, wanting to share this moment with her, but couldn't find her.

An official moved through the crowd and extended his hand to Drew. "Congratulations, Mr. Keelan. If you'll follow me, we'll get the paperwork all taken care of. You're going to the US Open!"

Drew couldn't believe it was happening. He kept shaking his head, as if trying to wake himself from a dream.

And where was Whitney? He wanted to hug her and kiss her and tell her that he couldn't have done it without her.

But as he moved into the clubhouse with his new entourage, he had no idea where she had gone.

Chapter Fourteen

Whitney didn't try to avoid Drew—but every time she wanted to get close to congratulate him, someone else was there, shaking his hand, taking a picture with him, or talking excitedly about the US Open, which was only four weeks away in Massachusetts.

She couldn't help but wonder where she would be in four weeks. Maybe in the Twin Cities, preparing to start teaching? Anywhere other than Timber Falls to see Drew and Heather together.

Whitney stood near the stage in the clubhouse ballroom where the sound crew was setting up for the evening festivities. Wonderful smells were coming from the kitchen as the staff prepped the meal that would soon be served. The ballroom, where Whitney was waiting to do a mic check, was abuzz with waiters filling water glasses, setting out bread baskets and prepping the wait stations.

Even with the activity, Whitney couldn't stop thinking about seeing Heather give Drew another hug when they'd realized he had taken third place in the qualifying round. Whitney had wanted to be by his side, to share in the moment with him—but had realized it was probably best that she wasn't. It would be Heather by his side after Whitney left, so why not start now?

Her insides were all twisted with the memory of seeing them together—and with the nerves that were threatening to make her sick whenever she thought about singing tonight.

If she thought performing at Cricket's wedding was a lot of pressure, it was nothing compared to the pressure she felt to sing for Drew on this special night. The ballroom seated three hundred people and every possible ticket had been sold for the event. It would be the largest gathering she'd ever sung for and, more than that, her performance would directly reflect on Drew.

She wasn't sure she could do it, but she didn't know what other choice she had. Drew had held up his end of the agreement and now she must hold up hers. To do otherwise would be unforgivable.

"Whitney?"

She turned at the sound of a deep voice and found Professor Perkins entering the ballroom. She'd remember him anywhere.

"There you are!" he said, his voice pleasant. "I was hoping to get a chance to speak to you before your performance tonight."

Horrible nerves filled Whitney until she began to shake, but she forced a smile and shook Sean's hand.

"Hello."

"It's nice to see you again. How long has it been since your sister's wedding?"

Whitney wanted to groan. Why was he bringing up the wedding? To remind her of her horrible performance? Surely he wouldn't be doing it on purpose if he'd come all this way to hear her again.

"The wedding was four years ago," she said.

"Sorry about your loss." He shook his head. "I can't imagine how hard it's been for you."

"Thanks." What else could she say? She didn't know how to put her loss into words, nor did she want to.

"I'm excited to hear you sing again. I remember how talented you were. I'm also looking forward to talking to you about your career. If we don't get a chance to this evening, perhaps we could meet for breakfast in the morning."

Whitney offered a wobbly smile. "I would like that."

"Good." He smiled. "Behind every great

student is an accomplished, talented and confident teacher. I believe you have what it takes."

She grew still as she stared at him. The pressure she'd felt before started to increase until panic rose up inside her, making her heart pound. She had to get out of the ballroom, to get some fresh air and fill her lungs.

"I'll do my best," Whitney said quickly. "I need to, um, I'll be right back." She started to back away from him. "I'll see you later."

"I look forward to it."

The need to flee was overwhelming, but as she left the ballroom and entered the lobby, there were so many people mingling she felt even more suffocated.

Outside beckoned, so she went toward the back of the clubhouse where a large deck overlooked the eighteenth hole and the Mississippi River beyond.

It felt good to inhale the fresh air. Even though there were several people standing on the deck, chatting, there was a lot more room to move and breathe.

"I've been looking all over for you." Drew exited the clubhouse and walked toward Whitney, as if he was afraid someone would try to stop him. "Where have you been?"

He looked so handsome, with his golfing attire, his windblown hair and the glow of his success radiating from his happy face.

"I've been here, but you've been awfully busy." She smiled, truly happy for him. "Congratulations."

He stopped in front of her, his eyes taking her in as if he hadn't seen her in weeks. "I couldn't have done it without you, Whitney."

"Yes, you could." She chuckled. "I didn't do anything."

"You encouraged me and challenged me to move beyond my fears—and I'm so happy you did." He put his hands on her arms, shaking his head in disbelief.

"I'm going to Massachusetts in a month to play in the US Open!"

"Oh, Drew." She went into his arms, giving him the hug she had wanted to give him since he learned he was in the top three. "I'm so proud of you."

He held her tight, lifting her until she was on her tiptoes. "I'm proud of you, too. I spoke to Sean and he's excited to hear you sing."

She closed her eyes, the anxiety returning as he set her down again and she took a step back.

Drew frowned and lowered his head to try to get her to look him in the eyes. "What's wrong, Whitney?"

She wouldn't show him her anxiety, wouldn't let him know how scared she was to sing tonight. A deal was a deal and she would do it, no matter how terrified she was.

Forcing herself to smile, she met his gaze. "Nothing."

"Is this about yester—"

"No." She put her hand on his chest to quiet him. "I don't want you to think about yesterday. Today is all about you and your success."

He put his hand over hers and she could feel his heart pumping hard. "I have thought of almost nothing else since yesterday." He lifted his other hand and put a tendril of hair behind her ear. "I wish we could clear the air now. I want you to know—"

"No." She shook her head, not wanting to ruin this perfect day. "Let's wait, Drew. I want to focus on your victory and on my performance tonight. I'm already shaking—I don't want to add more emotion to an already roller-coaster day."

"You're right." He took her hand into his and lowered it, but didn't let it go. "I shouldn't have brought it up yet. I needed my focus today and you need yours tonight. I won't mention it again. We can talk tonight, when everything is done."

"Thank you," she whispered.

"But can I say one thing?" he asked quietly.

She studied him, loving the way the sun shimmered in his blue eyes, reminding her of the river. "What?"

"Nothing we've done is a mistake, Whitney. Nothing." He lifted her hand and kissed it.

She inhaled at the touch of his lips against her skin.

Heather stepped out onto the deck and paused when she saw them.

Drew looked over his shoulder and lowered Whitney's hand, letting it go as he turned to face his assistant.

"Sorry," Heather said, though she didn't look sorry for interrupting them. "They need you for some photos, Drew."

"Okay. I'll be right there."

Heather looked at them for a split second longer and then returned to the clubhouse.

Drew glanced back at Whitney. "I saved you a spot next to me at the champions table for supper." He smiled. "Will you sit with me?"

Placing her hand on her queasy stomach, Whitney said, "I don't know if I'll have an appetite. I might spend the time warming up my voice out here."

Disappointment clouded his features. "There will be some speeches and some awards given—I couldn't think of anyone I'd want next to me more than you. Please?"

After all they'd been through, Whitney couldn't deny his request. "Okay—but I don't know if I'll eat anything."

"I just want you by my side."

She smiled again, his words warming her cheeks. "I'll be there."

"Thank you, Whitney." He leaned in and kissed her cheek, lingering for a second as she caught her breath.

When he pulled back, his smile was so bright she wanted to reach out and touch his face, but she refrained.

It was getting harder and harder to know if she was making the right choices.

The meal was delicious. The ballroom was perfect. And Whitney, sitting beside him, charming his tablemates, was the best part of his day.

It was exactly what they both needed. A way for them to relax and let go of all the anxiety and uncertainty they'd been feeling the past twenty-four hours.

At least, that was how Drew felt. He could tell that Whitney was getting more and more anxious to sing, and she hardly touched a thing on her plate, but she engaged in the conversation around the table and, more than once, Drew watched as the other men at his table admired her.

Just wait until they heard her sing.

"I should probably join the band on stage," Whitney said to Drew after all the awards had been handed out and the meal was being cleared away. "I'll need to start singing soon."

He put his hand on hers to steady her for a second as he looked into her eyes. "You're going to do an amazing job, Whitney. Just like you did at the park the other night. And I'll be here the whole time. Whenever you need a little encouragement or strength, you don't need to look any further than me."

She smiled and he had the urge to kiss her, right then and there, but he didn't. Kissing her hand and her cheek earlier was as much risk as he could take, for now. He wanted so much more, but would never push her, and would never share his first kiss with her in front of all these people.

No, their first kiss would be something special and private and for their hearts and eyes only.

"Are you leaving us?" one of the other golfers asked Whitney, disappointment on his face.

"I'm afraid I'm needed elsewhere,"

Whitney said as she stood. "I'm going to join the band."

"That's right," said another, "you're going to sing, aren't you?"

Whitney nodded. "For better or worse."

"She's being modest," Drew said as he smiled at her. "She's an amazing singer."

"How'd you ever win her over, Drew?" the first one asked. "She's one in a million."

Drew's chest expanded at the praise his wife was receiving and he shook his head. "I have no idea."

Whitney laughed and put her hand on his shoulder, her eyes more serious than her laughter.

"I'll see you later," she said to Drew.

"Wait." He stood and she stopped.

He leaned over and kissed her cheek again, pausing to say in her ear, "You look really pretty tonight, Whitney."

She pulled back and laid her hand on his face. "Thank you." And then she was gone.

After the tables were cleared by the banquet staff and moved to make a dance floor near the stage, Drew took a seat and watched as Whitney did a sound check with the band that had been hired for the evening.

There was a festive quality to the air. He still couldn't believe he was heading to the US Open in less than a month. It didn't seem possible, but he had done it.

"Well, Mr. Keelan," Heather said as she took the seat next to him. "How does it feel to have the hardest part of the day behind you?"

Drew glanced up at the stage right as Whitney looked his way. Their gazes collided and he could see the same apprehension in her eyes as he'd seen before she sang at the park, and earlier, when she'd watched Heather next him.

He thought about the conversation they needed to have tonight, and he wondered if the hardest part of his day *was* behind him. Though they'd had a good time during the meal, there was still that underlying tension between them, and he knew Whitney well enough to know that she hadn't forgotten about yesterday. Whatever Paula had said or done had somehow convinced Whitney that their entire marriage was a mistake.

Heather watched Drew, expecting him to answer, so he just smiled. "It feels good to have the tournament behind us so I can focus on the future."

Whitney glanced between Drew and Heather and then looked away.

He could tell her anxiety was starting to get the better of her—could see it in her eyes, in the way she held her shoulders, and in the way she clenched her hands into fists. He needed her to look at him, to know that she was going to be okay, but she didn't. She looked everywhere but at him.

Was it because of Heather?

Of course she'd be leery of his relationship with Heather. Why hadn't he realized it before now?

"I'm going to grab something to drink," he said as he stood and put some space between himself and Heather. "I'll see you later."

He went to the beverage cart near the door and filled a glass with water, though he wasn't thirsty.

"This has been a wonderful event," Sean said as he walked up to Drew. "Well done, all of it. I've been enjoying myself immensely. I can't wait for Whitney to sing."

Drew smiled and nodded. "I'm sorry we didn't have room for you at our table."

"I understand completely. I enjoyed meeting my tablemates. I dabble in golf a bit and spent the better part of an hour discussing the game with several players. It was very enlightening."

The band began to play the first few notes of a song and Whitney stepped up to the microphone. She smiled, though Drew could see it was a wobbly attempt.

He held his breath, hoping and praying she'd look his way.

Instead, she found Sean, and when she did, Drew could see the real panic set in. He'd seen it before, at Cricket and Sam's wedding—the pale skin, the glassy-eyed gaze and the shallow breathing.

The band played "Everything I Do, I Do It for You," but she didn't start singing when she was supposed to. Thankfully, the band kept playing. She looked back at them and Drew knew she was a split second away from leaving the stage.

Everyone was watching expectantly, so Drew did the only thing he could think to do. He walked out to the middle of the dance floor and caught her gaze when she turned back around.

She stared at him as she clutched the microphone stand and he gave her a slight nod, willing her to continue, knowing she had it in her. He believed in her, more than he believed in himself, and he knew she could do this.

Whitney swallowed and nodded back at him, and then she began to sing.

She didn't look to the left or to the right, but focused on him. It was just like at the park, only this time, it didn't take her as long to calm her nerves. Within just a few verses, she seemed to be in complete control of herself and her voice once again.

And as she sang, she smiled at him, allowing her voice to reach its full potential.

Drew knew the moment the room realized the talent that was before them. They quieted, all of them staring at her. Three hundred people, their gazes riveted to the stage.

Soon, people began to join Drew on the dance floor, and by the third song, "Shake It Off" by Taylor Swift, half of the room had come out to dance, Whitney was smiling, and Sean was tapping his foot to the tune.

Drew got drowned out by the others, but it didn't matter anymore. Whitney owned the stage—the whole room—and she was doing her thing without needing his help anymore.

She was amazing.

"I'm impressed," Sean said as he walked up to Drew. "She has one of the freshest voices I've heard in a long time. It's matured and improved since the wedding."

Drew could only smile, incredibly proud of his wife.

"I wonder why she's waited so long to put her skills to use," Sean continued. "If she can teach as well as she can sing, she has an amazing career ahead of her."

Even though Drew knew Whitney had it in her, he was still speechless.

"I'm eager to talk to her," Sean continued. "We have a position opening at the university and I would like to recommend her for the job."

The University of Minnesota was in the Twin Cities, a hundred miles away.

Drew couldn't speak for Whitney—but he wanted to tell Sean that Whitney lived in Timber Falls. What would she think of a job offer in the Twin Cities? Was it something she'd want?

Either way, it was part of her dream. It seemed strange that in the space of just one day, Drew had a chance to play in the US Open and she had a possible job offer. They'd pushed each other beyond their comfort zones and they were on the brink of achieving their dreams. What more might they do together? What summits could they climb?

Elliot would have two parents to look up to, two people who were willing to put it all on the line to reach for their dreams. What might Elliot dream of doing one day? Drew couldn't wait to find out.

But more than that, he was excited to finally talk to Whitney. Maybe, after all that they'd accomplished today, she would realize that their marriage wasn't a mistake, that God had brought them together for a unique purpose and He didn't make mistakes, even if they did.

Drew was counting down the hours until they could be home, alone, together.

Chapter Fifteen

By the end of the evening, Whitney was exhausted, but filled with a sense of accomplishment. She had finally mastered her fears and performed for Drew's event—an event that meant more to him than almost anything else. When she had first started, and her anxiety had almost sent her off the stage, he had appeared on the dance floor to assure her that she wasn't alone. And in that moment, she'd realized how much she loved Drew Keelan.

If she'd had his support and confidence during Cricket and Sam's wedding, she might not have panicked and ruined their ceremony, she might not have fought with her parents, and they might not have been estranged for the past four years.

Maybe.

The trouble with her parents extended back before the wedding.

But, either way, she had Drew's support now and it made all the difference.

Her heart had expanded when he stepped forward and she was fairly certain she would burst from pure joy. But then, she had watched him throughout the evening as he mingled with his guests, reminding her that they were two very different people, from two very different worlds. He was in his element in this room, with these people. And though she had enjoyed sitting with him during the meal, she had felt like an imposter. She would have been better suited to serving the meal than enjoying it with him and his friends. For years, she had tried fitting in at functions like this, but her parents had criticized her every move, often berating her at the end of an evening, listing all of the ways she had embarrassed them.

Her thoughts were putting a damper on her sense of accomplishment as she finished her last set, so she forced them away and accepted the applause of the audience.

The room became quieter, allowing the conversation to swell, as a few dozen people still remained.

"Thank you," Whitney said to the band as they began to clear their instruments from the stage.

"Thank *you*," said the lead guitarist. "We're happy to play with you whenever you'd like. You rocked it tonight."

Whitney smiled at his compliment and then turned to find Sean Perkins standing by the foot of the stage.

She walked down the steps and joined him on the dance floor. Though her performance was over, she was still nervous to speak to him. Would he know of a job for her? Have advice she could use?

He smiled. "I enjoyed your performance very much, Whitney. I would like to discuss your future plans, if you have the time. Perhaps tomorrow morning?"

Whitney's chest expanded. "I would like that."

"I want to know more about your education background and your qualifications, because we have a position opening up in the music department at the university next fall. If it's something you'd be interested in pursuing, I would be happy to recommend you to the faculty board."

"A position at the University of Minnesota?" Whitney put her hand to her throat. It was what she'd always wanted, wasn't it? To teach music? And at the University of Minnesota?

"There are a lot of things to discuss," Sean said. "But I think you have a lot of potential, Whitney. I'd like to mentor you and see where you take your talents."

"I'm honored." Whitney blinked a few times, trying to gather her thoughts. What would Drew think of this offer? Would he be proud of her? She hadn't seen him for thirty minutes or so—come to think of it, she hadn't seen Heather, either.

The joy Whitney felt came crashing down. If she took the position at the university, she would have to move to the Twin Cities—she'd have to leave Drew and Elliot—but wasn't that for the best? Hadn't she already decided that Drew and Elliot were better off without her? This was the best possible scenario, wasn't it?

Even though she knew this decision would be good for all of them, it didn't mean that her heart wasn't breaking. She loved Drew and Elliot more than life itself, but sometimes love meant sacrifice.

"I'm sure I've given you a lot to think about," Sean continued. "I'm staying at the Evanses' bed-and-breakfast tonight and plan to leave tomorrow afternoon. If you'd like to meet with me for breakfast, just send me a text." He handed her a business card with his number on it. "I'd love to talk to you about the future."

"Thank you." She accepted the card and looked at the number. "I'll let you know."

"Good." Sean smiled again and dipped his head before leaving the ballroom.

People were dispersing and the lights were flipped on so the banquet staff could finish cleaning the room.

Whitney had a lot to think about. But at the moment, she was afraid that if she went looking for Drew and found him with Heather, she might embarrass herself with her reaction. She'd never been the jealous type, but seeing Drew with his assistant did something inside Whitney that she didn't like. Confirming that her feelings for Drew had gone deep, very quickly.

It would be better to get back to Elliot and let Mrs. Topper go home. In the quiet house, she might be able to think clearly about what she needed to do next. Give herself a little space from Drew and the country club.

As she walked out of the ballroom, she was stopped by several people who congratulated her on a job well done. She received so many compliments her cheeks were hurting from smiling.

The night was cool as she stepped outside. A million stars sparkled above the golf course and the river running nearby. For a second, she just stood and admired God's creation, thinking about all the people who had been at the golf course that day, of the new friendships she was growing and the energy that had pulsed through the crowd.

If she was honest with herself, she had enjoyed every moment of it. For the first time in her life, she had felt like she belonged on the golf course. It was strange, since she'd spent most of her life hating it and all it implied. Without the constant scrutiny of her parents, she had been able to relax as she walked the course, watching Drew play a game she had always despised but was coming to appreciate. To see him play it was a completely different experience. He had treated it like an old friend, a companion, someone he knew intimately.

Whitney inhaled a long breath, drawing the cool air into her lungs. She couldn't help but admire the way the moon danced on the surface of the river, the gentle movement of the flag on the eighteenth hole, or the towering trees and well-manicured fairways. This course was a reflection of Drew and it was magnificent.

She got into the golf cart she had driven over to the clubhouse earlier that day and turned on the headlights to drive home.

Her mind was so full tonight, not only of what had happened, but of thoughts about the future, too. She had hoped that she would be certain about her next steps by the time she returned home, but she was more confused than ever.

Mrs. Topper was sitting in the living

room, reading a book, when Whitney entered the house.

"How was it?" she asked, her gentle face filling with keen excitement.

"It was wonderful," Whitney said. "Thank you so much for sitting with Elliot."

"He was a dream." She winked. "That's a special little boy, for sure."

Whitney started to pull cash out of her purse, but Mrs. Topper stilled her hand. "I wouldn't take it, even if you forced me. It was a gift to spend the day with him. That's all the payment I need. I'll do it any time."

"Thank you." Whitney smiled. "It was easy to relax today knowing he was in such capable hands."

"My pleasure." She went into the foyer and grabbed her purse. "Good night, dear."

"Good night." Whitney stood by the front door until Mrs. Topper got into her car and pulled out of the driveway.

It was very quiet in the house—too

quiet. Slowly, Whitney closed the door and then turned to look at the foyer.

Somehow, in the past two weeks, it had started to feel like home. Even now, as she kicked off her heels and set her purse on the table near the front door, she felt peaceful to be back in this little sanctuary. It still reminded her of Cricket every time she turned around—but it was starting to feel like Whitney's home, too.

How would she ever have the courage to leave it all behind?

An ache filled Whitney's chest as she climbed the stairs to check on Elliot, wondering when Drew might come home. Was he celebrating with Heather?

Elliot's muffled cry came through the closed door, telling her that he needed her—filling her with the same sense of accomplishment she'd felt earlier tonight when she'd been singing. Both roles gave her purpose and joy—but couldn't anyone meet Elliot's needs? There was nothing special about Whitney, after all.

She opened the door and peeked her head inside. The room was lit by a single night-light, offering just enough glow for Whitney to make her way across the thick carpet to Elliot's crib.

He was fussing, but hadn't started to cry hard—not yet.

"Hello," she said in a quiet, soothing voice.

Elliot opened his eyes and looked up at her. He stopped crying as he studied her face—and then he smiled.

It was the first time she'd seen him smile—really smile, his gums showing—and he looked so happy to see her, as if he'd missed her.

Tears filled Whitney's eyes as she returned the smile and reached into the crib and lifted him out. Love warmed her heart, filling her with the most indescribable emotions. She'd never known this feeling existed, and now that it did, she knew she'd never be the same again.

Elliot didn't fuss, but seemed completely content as she held him. Slowly, she walked over to the rocking chair and sat with him nestled into the crook of her elbow. He continued to look up at her as she started to rock him back and forth and sing "Lullaby," by Billy Joel.

He stared at her, his eyes lighting up with another smile. Whitney's heart broke a little more as she began to sing the next verse.

The songwriter promised to never leave the child he was singing to, but could Whitney make that promise to Elliot?

More importantly, could she keep it?

"Go home," Heather said to Drew as he stood behind the front desk looking over several invoices. "You've been here longer than the rest of us and you need to get some sleep. You'll have to start practicing around the clock if you want to be ready for the US Open."

Drew let out a weary sigh. He was excited, but exhausted. It had been a long day, and the truth was, all he wanted to do was take Whitney home and revel in their success. He also wanted to talk to her about what had happened yesterday and reassure her that no matter what Paula said, it didn't matter to him.

"I think I will," he said. "These invoices will be here tomorrow."

"I plan to be here early tomorrow morning," she said. "I can take care of them."

"Thank you for all your help. I've really appreciated that you've given it your all, even though you're leaving."

Heather shrugged and smiled. "I can't imagine doing anything different."

"See you tomorrow." He smiled and left the desk to find Whitney. He'd exited the ballroom about forty-five minutes ago to say goodbye to the officials who were leaving. He had heard the music stop, so he knew she would be ready to go home. No doubt she was just as tired as he was.

Visions of cuddling up with her by the fireplace warmed him, and all he could think about was getting her home. But would she want to be near him? He still had no idea how she felt about him.

When he entered the ballroom, they told him she had left about fifteen minutes ago. He looked in the restaurant and bar, but no one had seen her. One of the greenkeepers said that he saw her heading toward home in their golf cart.

Why had she left before him? Without telling him? Was something wrong with Elliot? Had Mrs. Topper called?

Drew found a golf cart and headed toward home All he could think about was getting to Whitney. The entire drive, his mind was filled with Whitney, though it was no surprise. She was all he could think about lately—no matter where he went. But right now, knowing how upset she'd been yesterday, and not being able to talk to her about it, made his pulse pick up speed. He longed to comfort her, to reassure her.

When he finally pulled up to the house,

his heart was beating hard. A single light was on in the foyer, but the rest of the house was dark.

Quietly, he entered the front door and listened to see if she was still awake.

Disappointment filled his chest at the thought of her going to bed before they could talk. He didn't want to have to wait until tomorrow morning. What he had to say needed to be said now.

A gentle sound came from upstairs and as Drew followed the sound, he realized it was Whitney, singing a lullaby.

The door was cracked open, allowing him to peek inside. Whitney was on the rocking chair, still wearing the gown she'd changed into for the dinner and dance. Her hair was in an updo, with tendrils teasing her cheeks. As she looked down at Elliot, and he looked up at her, there was something so tender and beautiful. Filled with a rush of affection, he leaned against the doorframe. He didn't think he could love either of these two any more than he did before, but he realized, in that moment, that love grew. It was never stagnant, but it expanded and filled all the bits and pieces of him that had been empty.

He loved Whitney Emmerson Keelan with all of his heart and soul and he wanted her to know, because he didn't think he could keep it inside for much longer.

Slowly, Elliot's eyes began to close and he was asleep as Whitney finished the song.

It was then that Whitney noticed Drew leaning against the doorframe, watching her.

Her eyes were full of something sweet and tender as she looked at him. He'd never wanted to kiss someone more than he did her—and if Elliot hadn't been in her arms, he was certain that he would have tried.

But would she let him? Did she return his feelings?

Dread and panic filled him at the thought that she didn't.

Whitney slowly stood and laid Elliot in the crib. Drew stayed by the door, not wanting to disturb his sleeping nephew.

After she laid him in his bed, she walked across the room.

Drew backed up into the hallway as Whitney closed the door behind her.

It was dim, with just a hint of light climbing up the stairs from the foyer. But Drew didn't need light to know what Whitney looked like. In just a couple of weeks, he already had her beautiful face memorized.

"Is everything all right?" he asked. "Why did you leave without me?"

"You were busy and I didn't want to bother you."

"Whitney, you could never be a bother to me." He wanted to draw her into his arms and reassure her, but there was much to be said. "You were magnificent tonight."

She looked down, and though it was dim, he could still make out her features enough to see that she was embarrassed by his praise.

"I'm so proud of you," he continued. "I might have qualified for the US Open today, but you were the one everyone is talking about on their way home tonight. I lost count of how many people came up to me to ask who you were—and I was so proud to tell each of them that you are my wife. Sean was so impressed—"

"He wants to meet tomorrow," she said. "He told me that there is a position opening at the University of Minnesota and he is thinking about recommending me for the job."

His heart felt like it paused in his chest. "What did you say?"

"I told him I would let him know." She shrugged. "It's a chance of a lifetime."

"You would have to move to the Twin Cities—wouldn't you?"

She looked at him, her brown eyes full

of so many questions and fears. "D-Don't you think it's best?"

"No." His answer was quick and certain. "I want you to follow your dreams and I would never stand in your way—but I don't want you to go, Whitney." He took a tentative step closer to her. "I want you to stay, here, with Elliot and me, for the rest of our lives."

"But didn't we agree that—?"

"That we'd let each other out of this marriage if something came up?" He reached out and took Whitney's hand in his own. "Has something come up? Have you decided you don't want to be married to me anymore?"

Whitney swallowed and looked down at their hands. "I—I don't think it has anything to do with what I want. I know what's best for you, Drew."

"Do you?" He drew her toward him until she was standing impossibly close. "Because I don't think you do—not if you're suggesting that you leave."

She bit her bottom lip as she regarded him, uncertainty in her face.

"Why do you think it would be best to leave?" he asked, trying desperately to resist pulling her the rest of the way so he could kiss her. "You said we should always be honest with each other, so I want to know. What happened yesterday? What did Paula say that made you so upset?"

Whitney took a deep breath. "She said that if I hadn't come along, you'd be married to Heather right now. She also said that I've never fit in anywhere and I've just embarrassed myself by trying." She shrugged. "And Paula is right. I didn't fit in before and I don't fit in now. But the truth is, I don't care if I embarrass myself—I only care about embarrassing you. It would destroy me if I knew I had hurt you in any way."

His heart broke for her and he shook his head. Gently, slowly, he lifted his hand to her soft cheek. "Whitney, you're not hearing the words coming out of my mouth. I'm proud of you—incredibly proud. You couldn't embarrass me, even if you tried."

He studied her beautiful face, hoping she would understand.

"Like I said before," he continued, "you were never willing to bend and conform to fit Paula's mold and that's what she hated the most." He ran his thumb along the ridge of her cheek, loving the feel of her beneath his skin. "You didn't fit your parents' mold or expectations, either, but that doesn't mean you didn't fit anywhere else."

Her face began to relax at his words and touch.

"God made you with a perfect plan in mind," Drew said, "forming you and designing you from His mold. Maybe your parents didn't plan on having you—but God did. Your arrival was designed from the formation of the Earth, regardless of your parents' plans. But to me, that means your life is precious because God chose you. Don't try to conform or worry about other people's expectations. Be the woman God created you to be."

Her eyes softened and filled with tears as her lips turned up into a tender smile.

"And," he said as he finally pulled her into his arms, reveling in the feel of her so close, her body conforming to the dips and swells of his own. "I firmly believe that God created you and me for each other. *We* fit perfectly." To prove his point, Drew lowered his lips to kiss her.

She tilted her face up to receive his kiss, matching his desire with her own. She wrapped her arms around his neck, pulling him closer.

Their breath mingled, filling Drew with pleasure and joy. Her kiss was both sweet and passionate, and he knew, without a doubt, that she cared for him, too.

Drew couldn't believe that this was his wife—that this beautiful, talented, kind, selfless woman was his bride. He longed for her to be his wife in every sense of the word, but he needed her to know he loved her.

And he wanted to know if she loved him in return.

It took all his willpower to break the kiss, and when he did, they were both breathless.

"I love you," he whispered to her as their foreheads were pressed together. "I love you with all of my heart, Whitney. I don't want you to leave. I want you to stay and be my wife. I want to create a real family with Elliot—and maybe, if God so chooses, we'll have other children one day."

Whitney pulled back—and for a heart-breaking second, he was afraid she'd tell him she didn't want the same thing.

But the smile she offered him was so glorious he couldn't imagine her saying anything that could break his heart.

"I love you, too," she whispered. "So very much, Drew. I didn't think it was possible, because it hasn't been that long— but maybe you're right, maybe our love grew so quickly because God made us for each other."

He smiled, and though it was late, and he'd had a big day, he had never had so much energy in his life.

"Do you really mean what you said?" she asked him. "About me?"

Drew put his hands on either side of her face and kissed her again, deeply and passionately. "I meant every single word."

"And you don't think marrying me was a mistake?"

"I've never been surer of anything than our marriage, Whitney. I'm yours, forever, if you want me."

She laughed and threw her arms around him, hugging him close. "I do want you, very much."

He lifted her off her feet and returned her hug. In one day, he had realized two of his greatest dreams.

He was going to the US Open and he had found the woman he planned to spend the rest of his life loving.

Chapter Sixteen

The day was bright and glorious as Drew held Whitney's hand and smiled at her. They were in the car, heading through Timber Falls, with Elliot in his car seat in the back. All the familiar businesses passed by as Whitney let out a content sigh.

It had been two weeks since the tournament at the golf course, and the day Drew had told her he loved her. The time had passed by in a blur, yet Whitney felt as if a decade had passed. She loved Drew more than ever before, making her feel as if they'd been a little family for much longer than four weeks.

So much had already happened. Whitney had turned down the offer to work for the university, and, instead, Drew had helped her start up her own music school in Timber Falls and she already had several students.

Between teaching, caring for Elliot, and supporting Drew, her life was full and happy.

"Where are we going?" Whitney asked Drew as he took a right onto Broadway. "We have so much packing to do if we're going to leave town tomorrow."

They planned to drive from Timber Falls, by way of Niagara Falls, to enjoy a short honeymoon on their way to the US Open in Massachusetts. It had been a big question whether or not they would take Elliot, but they had both decided that they didn't want to leave the baby behind. He would be with them, so it would be their first family vacation, as well.

Paula still took Elliot one day a week, though Drew and Whitney had confronted her after the incident at the grocery store. Drew had been adamant that if Paula couldn't accept Whitney as his wife—and Elliot's mother—then she would not have a place in their life. Since then, Paula had kept her thoughts and feelings to herself and had offered Whitney and Drew a little respite in their week. Whitney hoped that as time passed, they might start to heal the rift between them, though she never expected them to be close.

Civil and kind was all she really cared about.

"I'm not sure how much more you could pack for our trip," Drew teased her. "You've already filled three suitcases full."

"I don't know what Elliot might need." She shrugged. "I've never traveled with an infant before."

He squeezed her hand and smiled at her again. "We can always buy whatever we might forget. We're going to Canada, not the Amazon."

She playfully rolled her eyes—but knew he was right. "You still didn't answer my question," she reminded him. "Where are we going right now? And why is it a secret?"

"You'll see." He lifted her hand and kissed the back. "If I tell you, it won't be a surprise and I've been working on this for a couple weeks. We're almost there."

She looked around, but had no idea where they might be going. The courthouse was to her right and a hardware store was on her left. Up ahead was the Timber Falls Community Church and the library.

Whitney decided to be content with a surprise, especially since her husband had been the one to plan it.

He took a left on Third Street and pulled into the church parking lot, which was full. It was Saturday, so she didn't expect there to be so many cars. Perhaps there was a school program going on, since the Christian School was attached to the back of the church.

But why would Drew be taking her to a school program? And what school program was offered in June? Maybe a Vacation Bible School?

"What's going on here?" she asked him, turning her curious gaze toward her husband.

He just smiled, looking handsome today with his hair freshly cut and his face clean-shaven. He'd spent the past two weeks practicing for the US Open and was golfing better and better every day. Max and Piper were flying out to meet them in Massachusetts next week. Max was serving as Drew's caddy, and they were bringing along Max's mom, Mrs. Evans, who would take care of Lainey and Elliot at their Airbnb while the adults attended the tournament. It would be a long four days of golf as they followed Drew and Max, but Whitney was excited.

Knowing she'd have Piper with her made her all the more so.

Drew parked the car and turned to face Whitney. "Ready?"

"For what?" she asked.

"To get married—again."

Whitney frowned. "What do you mean?"

Drew reached into his pocket and pulled out a beautiful diamond ring. It caught the reflection of the sun, causing it to sparkle and shine. "Will you do me the honor of attending our wedding today?"

"Drew!" Tears instantly sprang to her eyes—tears of happiness and joy. She hadn't expected a ring, though she'd wanted one.

He slipped the cool, gold band over her ring finger. It fit perfectly.

"The church ladies helped me pull it all together," Drew said. "And Piper and Liv planned the ceremony and reception, decorating the church and ballroom at the clubhouse. Kate is going to sing for us and everyone else pitched in to provide all the details I didn't think about. Ed and his chamber orchestra will play tonight for the dance and the chef at the clubhouse has been planning an extensive menu."

"Truly?" Whitney shook her head. "You went to all this trouble for me?"

"Our courthouse wedding and our commitment to each other was enough," Drew assured her, "but I wanted to give my bride the wedding she deserves. I hope you like it."

"I love it—"

"It hasn't happened, yet."

"It doesn't matter. I know I'll love it." She leaned over and kissed him, setting her hand on the side of his face, catching the sparkle from her ring in the corner of her eye. "Thank you."

"Come on," he said. "Everyone's waiting."

"But I'm not dressed for a wedding," she said.

He winked at her. "It's all been taken care of. Piper thought of everything. Apparently, Max gave her a surprise wedding, too."

Whitney's chest was filled with such pleasure that she felt choked up, unsure if she'd be able to speak clearly throughout the event.

Drew took Elliot and his car seat out of the back of the car. He was sleeping as Drew handed the baby over to Whitney. Then he went to the trunk and pulled out a suit wrapped in a plastic garment bag.

"It wasn't easy getting this in here without you seeing it," he said to her with a laugh. "I'm actually surprised we were able to pull all of this off without you knowing. It hasn't been easy and you almost found out a couple of times."

Whitney couldn't stop smiling. "I'm happy I didn't. This is the sweetest thing anyone has ever done for me."

He kissed her again, loving the feel of her lips beneath his. "I plan to spend the rest of my life doing nice things for you, Whitney."

They entered the back of the church and were immediately greeted by Piper and Max.

"Surprise!" Piper said as she gave Whitney a hug. "Did you have any idea?"

"None." Whitney laughed as Mrs. Evans took Elliot to bring him to the church nursery.

"We'll have him in the sanctuary for the ceremony," she promised. "But you have a few things to do beforehand."

"Kiss your groom goodbye," Piper instructed, "because he won't see you again until the ceremony begins."

Whitney did as she was instructed, giving Drew a tight hug and a quick kiss, before Piper led her off to the women's restroom.

"I didn't know your style," Piper said, "so do you remember a couple weeks ago when we went shopping downtown and I stopped by the dress shop window and we pointed out our favorite styles?"

Whitney's mouth cracked open as she nodded in surprise. "I do!"

"Drew instructed me to return and purchase the gown you liked, because he didn't want to see it until it was on you. Then, he went into Cricket's closet and found the dress you wore for your first wedding and brought it to the shop so they could try to get some measurements for you. I hope it fits."

Piper opened the door and the first thing Whitney saw was the dress, hanging in the doorway.

And it was absolutely gorgeous. It was simple, with clean lines and a full skirt, with long-sleeves and a neckline that would lie low on her shoulders.

"I hope you like it," Piper said, clenching her hands together.

"I love it." Whitney couldn't believe they'd gone to so much trouble for her. "It's perfect."

"Good." Piper let out a relieved breath. "I chose a simple veil for you and my hairstylist is waiting to put your hair up and do your makeup. There's also a photographer, but he'll take pictures during the wedding and then go with us to the golf course and get more pictures there, along the river."

"It's all too much," Whitney said, overwhelmed in the best possible way. "You and everyone else shouldn't have gone to so much trouble."

"You deserve it," Piper said, putting her hands on Whitney's shoulder. "Both you and Drew deserve a happily-ever-after, and we're all here to get it started."

"Thank you doesn't seem enough," Whitney said, taking Piper's hand into her own. "How can I ever repay you?"

"You don't need to repay me," she said. "My friends gave me a beautiful wedding, and now I'm paying it forward. Someday, you can do the same. And I'm sure you will."

Whitney hugged Piper and grinned. "I will."

An hour later, with her hair up in curls and tendrils framing her face, Whitney looked at herself in the mirror. She was wearing the dress, which fit perfectly, and stared at her reflection, thinking of her sister's wedding day. Their mom and Cricket had planned everything, to the most minor detail. It had been exhausting to watch them. But on the day of the wedding, as their mother had stood by Cricket to look at her in her dress, her sister had been radiant and their mother triumphant.

Whitney wished that her mom and sister were with her now. She wasn't sure if her mother would have looked at her the way she looked at Cricket, but she might have been pleased, at the very least.

It was days like today that caused Whitney to mourn what could have been, or should have been.

But today wasn't for mourning or looking back. It was for looking forward and healing.

Piper entered the room with a flower

box. "Your husband just had these delivered."

With a smile, Whitney lifted the lid and found a dozen red roses in a bouquet.

"They're magnificent," she breathed.

Nodding her agreement, Piper lifted them out and handed them to Whitney. "I think everything's ready. Are you?"

She'd never been readier in her life.

They left the dressing room and entered the fellowship hall just outside the sanctuary. When Piper nodded at the two young boys standing by the doors, they opened them, revealing the sanctuary, which was full of guests. Several of the people in attendance were church members, but there were a few family members and old friends, as well.

"I'm sorry," Piper said, "but Drew didn't know if you wanted anyone to walk you down the aisle."

"That's okay," Whitney said. "I'm used to being on my own."

Mendelssohn's "Wedding March" drifted

out to Whitney as she stepped up to the opening—and that was when she saw Drew. Looking handsome in his suit, he was standing at the front of the church with Pastor Jacob.

For as long as she lived, she would never forget the look on his face when he saw her—it made her heart swell to bursting.

But when he stepped off the altar and walked toward her, she felt her heart start to pound with excitement.

She waited for him to reach her side at the back of the church, and when he did, he smiled, his eyes full of love and admiration. "I don't want you to have to take another step by yourself," he said, offering his arm. "From this moment forward, we'll be by each other's side, to have and behold, for better or worse, for richer or poorer, in sickness and in health, to love and to cherish, until God calls us home."

"Promise?" she whispered.

"Promise."

And, with that, they walked into the

church together, side by side, to make their marriage commitment in front of their family and friends.

Clouds hovered over the golf course on the fourth and final day of the US Open as Whitney stood on the edge of the seventeenth hole, Piper at her side. Both Whitney's and Piper's cheeks and noses were kissed by the sun after being outside for the past four days. They had watched a lot of golf and attended several evening events. But yesterday, when Drew had come up from behind to take third place on the leaderboard, the activities had increased. Suddenly, everyone wanted to know who he was, where he was from, and whom he was married to. Dozens of reporters had contacted them and Drew had been busy with interviews.

In the past twenty-four hours, Whitney had seen him for less than an hour before they'd crashed into bed in their Airbnb.

But now, as the crowd hushed and Drew

stood on the seventeenth green, eyeing up the hole for a birdie shot, Whitney held her breath. If he made the eight-foot putt, then he would be tied for first place, with one hole left to play.

She wasn't sure if God cared about the outcome of the US Open, but she knew that He cared for her and Drew, so she said a prayer for her husband. That no matter what, he would be happy with the result of the day.

Without realizing what she was doing, Whitney grabbed Piper's hand and squeezed it tight.

Piper returned the squeeze and let out a low breath.

Drew poised himself over the ball and took a couple of practice swings before he repositioned himself and hit the ball. It slowly rolled down the green toward the hole—and dropped in!

The crowd erupted with a wild shout and Whitney joined them, proud of her husband and awed by his calm demeanor.

Reaching down into the cup, Drew grabbed his ball and then tossed it to Max, who gave him a high five before they moved toward the eighteenth, and final, hole.

Before he disappeared with the crowd, and all the cameras, Drew turned to look for Whitney. When he caught her eye, he winked at her and she grinned.

Their honeymoon had been amazing as they'd driven around the Great Lakes, through Ontario, Canada, and dropped down into Niagara Falls. They had taken a couple of days to make the sixteen-hour drive, enjoying the time together in the car. Talking about anything and everything. Thankfully, Elliot had slept most of the way and they'd been able to stop often to feed him and change his diaper.

After spending a day at the falls, they'd headed east toward Brookline, Massachusetts, where the tournament would take place. Max and Piper were there at the Airbnb they'd rented, and the men had spent several days on the course preparing for the tournament while Whitney, Piper and Mrs. Evans had explored the Boston area with the children.

And then the tournament had started that Thursday. There were four rounds of golf, one each day, and the lowest score at the end of the four days would be the winner. Already, with the attention Drew had been getting, there was talk about him joining the PGA tour, but so much would depend on what happened today.

"This is it," Piper said as they followed the crowds moving toward the eighteenth hole. Whitney had already been told that a place would be saved for her and Piper near the eighteenth green, but she wanted to see Drew tee off and follow along on the hole.

"I can't believe how fast it all happened," Whitney said. "It's almost impossible to believe that he's about to play his last hole in the US Open."

"It might be his last hole in this tournament, but I am convinced he'll have dozens of other tournaments in his future."

"If that's what he wants..." Whitney let the comment trail off, because she knew it was what he wanted—what they both wanted—but she was hesitant to trust that it would happen. They both had so many dreams that a part of her struggled to believe they were coming true.

With Drew's help, Whitney had started to rent a charming building in downtown Timber Falls for her music school. She had dreams of expanding one day, but for now she was content. As her music school grew, she would reassess her dreams and allow them to ebb and flow naturally.

Just like all of her dreams.

A few minutes later, they were near the tee box and watched as Drew hit his last drive of the tournament. It flew straight and far—impossibly far—making Whitney wonder at this husband of hers.

The clouds were low and gray, threatening to rain. Whitney prayed the weather would hold off. Up until today, they'd enjoyed picture-perfect June weather. The wind had picked up a little, which would affect their play, but Drew knew what he was doing and she forced herself not to worry. If anyone had been born to play this game, it was him.

The crowd clapped for Drew and then watched as his golfing partner took his shot. The crowd held their breath and then let out a low moan as the ball sliced to the left, landing in a grove of trees.

Whitney didn't want to celebrate someone else's mistake, but she couldn't help feeling a little excitement for Drew. This gave him the opportunity to pull ahead.

They followed along and watched as Drew hit his second shot, landing his ball on the fringe of the eighteenth green—within shot of a birdie, which would place him one stroke back from the other top golfer.

And it would make him the winner.

The other golfer took two swings to

get to the green and Drew had to wait for him. Whitney and Piper found their places close to the green, within sight of Drew. Max gave Drew his putter and then he picked up the golf bag and moved over to stand near Whitney and Piper.

"Can he do it?" Whitney asked Max on a whisper.

"Definitely," Max said with a confident smile.

Whitney wished she felt so sure. She believed in her husband, but she also knew that anything could go wrong.

When it was finally time for Drew to make his shot, the hundreds of people standing around the green and watching in the stands waited in complete silence.

A bird twittered overhead, the wind whistled through the viewing stands and someone coughed.

Drew stood over his ball, looking at a ten-foot putt uphill. He and Max had already analyzed it from every direction, so Drew took his position above the ball, wiped his hands on his pant legs and then gripped his putter.

Whitney wanted to both close her eyes and keep them peeled open. She clutched her hands and lifted them up to her lips, breathing a prayer as Drew hit the ball.

As if in slow motion, the ball rolled up-hill toward the hole—straight and true. For a split second, it hovered at the edge of the cup, and then it tipped inside.

The crowd erupted in a cheer unlike anything Whitney had ever heard in her life.

Drew pumped his arms in the air and Max sprinted across the green to give him a bear hug. They were both grinning from ear to ear, but before Drew could join Whitney to celebrate, they had to wait for the other golfer to finish his hole.

After he did, and he was still one stroke behind Drew, Whitney was told by a volunteer that she could break the barrier. She did, without hesitation, and sprinted toward Drew, throwing her arms around him.

He lifted her off her feet, embracing her with such strength it took her breath away. "Congratulations," she said to him, pulling back to give him a kiss, almost forgetting that the cameras were probably watching them and people all over the world could see them. "I'm so proud of you, Drew."

"Thank you." He grinned, his handsome face glowing with happiness. "I'm so happy you're here with me, Whitney."

"So am I." Sooner than she wanted, she had to let him go since he needed to follow the officials to the clubhouse to get his scorecard authorized and conduct interviews with several national media reporters.

It was hours later, when they were finally alone together back at the Airbnb, that Whitney felt like they could both take a deep breath.

Elliot was asleep and the Evanses were in their own part of the large house.

The rain had started to fall and Drew

had turned on the gas fireplace to take the chill out of the air. They were sitting together on an oversize chair, their feet propped up on the ottoman, cuddling. Whitney was lying against Drew's chest, her right hand entwining with his left one where he wore the wedding band he had chosen for her to give to him on their wedding day.

Rain splashed against the windowpane, making Whitney thankful to be inside, warm and safe with Drew.

"It's been a big month," Drew said, his voice a bit lazy as his thumb ran over hers.

"A life-changing month." They'd been married for six weeks, but it had only been four weeks since they'd declared their love for one another and started living as man and wife.

"It's a pretty incredible way to start our lives together," he mused as he kissed the top of her head. "Do you think we'll get bored when life goes back to normal?"

She smiled and shook her head, ready to

share a secret she'd known all week, but hadn't wanted to say until after the US Open was done.

"If you think that having a one-year-old and an infant is normal, then I suppose we won't get bored."

Drew sat up, taking her with him. He stared at her. "Are you—?"

"Pregnant?" She nodded, hardly believing it herself.

His mouth parted as he studied her, awe and wonder on his face. "A baby?"

"Another one, yes." She couldn't help but grin. "I'm only a few weeks along. Do you mind?"

"Mind?" He pulled her close, hugging her tighter than he had when he'd won the tournament. "I couldn't be happier, Whitney."

Neither could she.

* * * * *

*If you liked this story from
Gabrielle Meyer,
check out her previous
Love Inspired books:*

A Mother's Secret
Unexpected Christmas Joy
A Home for Her Baby
Snowed in for Christmas
Fatherhood Lessons
The Soldier's Baby Promise

*Available now from Love Inspired!
Find more great reads at
www.LoveInspired.com.*

Dear Reader,

I love marriage-of-convenience stories, but they are a little harder to write in a modern setting. As I thought about how I could accomplish this, the idea for *The Baby Proposal* was born. I enjoyed creating Drew, Whitney and baby Elliot, named after my cousin's son. I also loved incorporating the game of golf into the story. My husband is an avid golfer and we live near a golf course, so it was fun to share the bits and pieces of the game that I love. I hope you enjoyed it, too!

Blessings,
Gabrielle Meyer